THE BiG WiSH

A MESSAGE FROM CHICKEN HOUSE

Make a wish! And another! And another! And another! What could go wrong? Well, maybe getting what you wish for doesn't always turn out to be what you really want. Brandon Robshaw tries it all out in his funny and rather revealing story of the boy who has it all.

Here I go, I wish for . . . Oh, no, I didn't mean it! Urghh!

BARRY CUNNINGHAM
Publisher
Chicken House

THE BiG WiSH

BRANDON ROBSHAW

Chicken House

2 Palmer Street, Frome, Somerset BA11 1DS
www.doublecluck.com

Text © Brandon Robshaw 2015
First published in Great Britain in 2015
Chicken House
2 Palmer Street
Frome, Somerset BA11 1DS
United Kingdom
www.doublecluck.com

Cover and interior design by Steve Wells
Typeset by Dorchester Typesetting Group Ltd
Printed and bound in Great Britain by CPI Group (UK) Ltd, Croydon CR0 4YY
The paper used in this Chicken House book is made from wood grown in sustainable forests.

1 3 5 7 9 10 8 6 4 2

British Library Cataloguing in Publication data available.

PB ISBN 978-1-908435-89-7
eISBN 978-1-910002-43-8

CHAPTER ONE

People often talk about having butterflies in their stomachs. Butterflies? With me it was . . . bees! Bats! Birds! Lobsters, snapping their claws!

It was a bright morning in early September and I was all kitted out in my brand-new school uniform: dark-grey trousers and blazer, white shirt, tie with diagonal red, black and white stripes. New black shoes without a scuff on them. Two-day-old haircut. My Adidas shoulder bag had a new calculator in it, along with a collection of pens, a geometry set and my packed lunch, which consisted of a cheese-and-coleslaw sandwich, an orange and a fruit-and-nut cereal bar.

I was sitting in the kitchen, trying to eat my toast. The sun was streaming through the window, the radio was on and the DJ sounded insanely cheerful. 'Happy Monday, everyone!' and all that. It was all right for him. All *he* had to do was lounge about in a studio, play records, burble on and get paid shed-loads of money for it. He didn't have to go to a great big massive new school with a thousand kids in it.

All bigger than him.

'Are you all right?' my mum said. She always knows when I've got something on my mind. It's like she's telepathic. 'Not too worried?'

'He should be!' said Maeve. 'They'll eat him alive!'

Ben was so shocked he stopped scratching his head. 'Eat him alive? They'll go to prison if they eat him alive!'

'It's just an expression,' Mum said. 'Don't worry, Sam. They won't eat you alive.'

'You don't know the place like I do, Mum,' said Maeve. She finished there last year and she's about to start sixth-form college. 'There are some real psychos.'

'Be quiet!' said Mum. 'Don't be so mean! Don't you worry about those psychos, Sam. Just keep out of their way.'

'Oh, yeah, that's a really good idea, Mum,' I said. Touch of sarcasm there, you know.

'Oh, come here!' Mum said, and she got up and hugged me, pressing me to her like I was a really little kid again. Only in those days my head only came up to her waist and now it was almost level with hers. And for a moment I wished I *was* a little boy again, with nothing to do except swing on swings and dig in sandpits and play with my toys and eat sweets and watch CBeebies . . .

There was a rap at the door.

'That'll be Evan,' I said.

He was standing there on the doorstep in his Mary Seacole Comprehensive School uniform. It was his big brother's cast-off uniform – the trousers ended way above his ankles, the sleeves of the jacket ended way above his wrists, and it wouldn't do up at the front. Evan's a bit overweight. Not actually *fat*. Just . . . well, he's in shape, and the shape is round, as my dad would say.

'What are you staring at?' Evan said. 'Do I look

really stupid?'

'No, no, no,' I said quickly. 'You look fine. Uber-cool.'

'No need to be sarcastic.' He sounded a bit huffy.

I wished I'd kept my mouth shut. Except – a funny thing – now Evan looked so worried, I felt a lot less worried myself. I'd handed on the worry-baton, like in a relay.

Mum came out into the hall. 'Hello Evan. Good luck, you two!'

Maeve appeared behind her. 'They'll need it!'

'*You* survived it there, didn't you?' said Mum.

'Yeah, just about!' said Maeve.

Anyway, we set off up the road, me and Evan. Mum stood at the gate and called out, 'Make some wise choices!' She's always said that, ever since I started primary school. She thinks it's funny. But it's just annoying.

Parents don't always know the difference.

Mary Seacole Comprehensive is a massive new building. Mostly yellow, with steel girders on the outside, and between the yellow walls there are sheets of glass you can see the staircases through.

'Weird, isn't it,' I said to Evan, as we stood outside. Hundreds of kids streamed past, jostling us as they went by. 'We've gone from being the biggest kids to being the smallest kids.'

'Yeah,' said Evan. 'Like in *Gulliver's Travels*. When he goes from Lilliput, where everyone's tiny and he's the giant, to Brobdingnag, where everyone's a giant and he's the tiny one.'

Evan says stuff like that all the time. And he hadn't just seen the film, either. He'd read the book, you could be sure about that.

'Yeah,' I said. 'I guess.'

'But it's going to be OK,' Evan said. 'Remember what Mrs Protheroe said – about the school's strict anti-bullying policy?'

'That's right,' I said. 'There's nothing to worry about.'

We looked at each other. 'Well,' Evan said, 'we'd better get in there.'

We knew where to go. They'd shown us on the Induction Day. We were in Mrs Protheroe's class in Room G11 on the ground floor. But there'd only been year sevens there then. It was all nice and quiet. Today it was like entering a giant beehive.

'You sure this uniform looks OK?' Evan said.

'Well, er, yeah,' I said. 'Totally.'

'Your hair's sticking up.'

'I know,' I said. 'I like it like that.'

So we went in and found our way through the noisy, crowded corridors to Mrs Protheroe's room, and went off to our first class, which was English with Mr Swaledale, and do you know what? Nothing bad or scary happened at all.

Until break time.

Me and Evan were kind of ambling along the side of this tarmacked area where some of the big kids were playing football. We were talking about who was the best ever Captain in *Captain Invincible*.

'Matt Lukovitz is good,' I said. 'He's funny. But I think I gotta say Garrett Butcher, on the whole, 'cause—'

'My dad says Sidney Kronk was the best.'

This put me in a bit of a dilemma. I'd seen an old *Captain Invincible* episode with Sidney Kronk in it and I wasn't that impressed. But I didn't want to sound as if I was contradicting Evan's dad, who's really ill. He's been in and out of hospital for the last two years having all sorts of treatments and operations, and he can't work any more. So I felt like it would be bad manners, if you know what I mean, to start saying that Evan's dad was all wrong about Sidney Kronk. Before I had a chance to work out what to say, a football came whizzing towards us at about a hundred-and-fifty miles an hour and smashed Evan right in the face, knocking his glasses off.

'Oi!' shouted a really horrible voice. 'Give us our ball back, you muppet!'

A tall kid with a pale face, black hair and cold, hard eyes was glaring at us.

Evan was on his hands and knees looking for his glasses. Blood trickled from his nose. I picked up the glasses and gave them to him.

'The ball! Kick it here, you little jerk!'

'Aren't you even going to say sorry?' I said. 'You just whacked him in the face.'

'He should keep his ugly face out of the way then!'

His mates were all laughing. But the boy himself didn't look like he thought it was funny at all. He started walking towards us. I threw the ball back, but he ignored it.

'What's your problem?' he said.

'You are.' It just sprang to my lips. I knew it was suicidal, but it was *true*.

He opened his eyes wide. He was right close-up in front of us now.

'You what? You *what*?'

He made a sudden movement with his hand like he was going to hit me. I jumped to one side, but then he casually moved his hand up and smoothed back his hair. His mates burst out laughing.

'Who are they letting in to this school these days? Look at this pair of doughnuts. *This* one' – he poked Evan really hard in the stomach, you could see his finger push right in – 'is so fat he couldn't get a uniform to fit him! And *this* one' – he poked me in the ribs and it really hurt – 'has hair like a bogbrush. A ginger bogbrush!'

His mates laughed even more and came closer, crowding around us. I gave Evan a kind of helpless look at the exact moment he turned and did the exact same look to me.

'What's your name?' said the tall boy.

'Evan Carter,' muttered Evan.

'What? Evan Farter?'

Cue gales of laughter from his mates. Evan went red.

'And you?' He turned on me. 'What's your stupid name?'

'Why? What's yours?'

I don't know why I was acting like I had a death wish. I have this idea that life should be *fair*, you know? If he could ask me my name, why couldn't I ask him his? I know life *isn't* fair – grown-ups are always coming out with that one – but it *should* be.

There was a gasp from his mates. 'You better teach him a lesson, Scorpus.'

Scorpus gave a sneering grin – like a bit of string was pulling his lip up on one side. 'Yeah, 'cause that's what school's for, innit? Learning lessons.' He pushed me right back against the wall. I could feel the bricks scraping against my vertebrae. And I wished, more strongly than I'd ever wished for anything in my life, that I had super-powers, like in Marvel comics. If I was Spiderman, I could punch him to the ground using all my spider-strength, and then tie him up in a web. Or if I was the Incredible Hulk, I could hurl him right across the playground and he'd go splat against the far wall. Or if I was the Mighty Thor, I'd get out my hammer and—

'You gotta pay *tax*,' Scorpus said. 'For being cheeky. Give us your money.'

'Leave him alone!' said Evan. 'This school has an anti-bullying policy—'

Hurricane of laughter.

Scorpus held his hand out in front of me. 'Dinner money.'

'I haven't got any, I brought a packed lunch.'

One of his mates – a thickset boy with a dyed-blond streak in his hair and a piercing in his eyebrow, even though that was against the rules – upended my Adidas bag. The calculator, geometry set and pens tumbled out, plus the lunch box.

'Oh, what we got here?' Scorpus picked up the calculator and geometry set. 'He's got all his little instruments, sweet or what?' He slipped them into his jacket pocket.

'Give those back!'

'Er, how can I put this? No.' Then he opened the lunch box. 'What we got here? Cheese? I hate cheese.' He dropped the sandwich on the floor and ground it under his heel, and all the coleslaw came splurting out the sides. He threw the orange up and down a couple of times, then pulled back his arm and sent it whizzing right across the playground. It splatted on the wall on the far side, just like he'd have done if I'd been the Incredible Hulk. Finally he took the cereal bar, looked at it, and slipped it into his other pocket. It was a chocolate-coated one.

'That's the end of the lesson,' Scorpus said. 'The lesson is, show some *respect*. You get me?'

All I had to do was say OK, or even just nod. But somehow . . . I just couldn't. I was scared of him. But I didn't respect him. So I just stared back dumbly.

'I *said*, d'you *get* me?'

'Oh, come on,' said one of Scorpus' mates. 'Let's get on with the game, the bell's gonna go soon.' He was a black kid with a shaved head, and even though he looked seriously hard, something in his voice gave me the idea he'd started to feel a bit sorry for me.

Scorpus turned to look at him. 'I'll "come on" when I'm ready, all right?'

'Look – a teacher's coming!' Evan said.

I felt a surge of relief as I saw a bald teacher with glasses and a brown corduroy jacket walking our way.

Scorpus swore. 'OK, let's play football. You two' –

he fixed us each in turn with a laser beam-stare – 'if you say anything, you're *dead*.' He drew his finger across his throat. 'Capeesh?'

'What?' I said. 'I don't know what *capeesh* means.'

Scorpus took half a step forward and for a second I thought he was going to start on me again. But the teacher was close now. Shaved-Head pulled Scorpus's arm, and Scorpus finally slouched away.

'Whew!' Evan said shakily. 'That was horrible!'

'What are we going to do?'

'Well . . . you can share my packed lunch.'

'Thanks. But I meant, we'll have to tell, won't we?'

'Will we?'

'Yeah, Mrs Protheroe said—'

'Yeah, but *he* said—'

'Yeah, but Mrs Protheroe said—'

'Yeah, but he'll kill us!'

'He won't,' I said. 'They won't let him.'

'How'd you know?'

'Look, they've got an anti-bullying policy. They have to, like, enforce it. Anyway, why should we let him get away with pushing us about like that and stealing my things? It's not fair!'

'Life's not fair,' said Evan.

'Well, we'll have to try and make it fair, then,' I said.

So we went to Mrs Protheroe and dropped Scorpus right in the poo.

And dropped ourselves in it too, as it turned out.

CHAPTER TWO

hen I got home from school, my mum asked, 'How was your first day?' etc, etc. I said it was fine. I didn't want to explain about Scorpus and his gang. It made me feel embarrassed, even though it wasn't my fault.

I was seriously worried about going back to school the next day. Mrs Protheroe had got us together with Scorpus and made him give the stuff back, which he did, with his face fixed in a sneer. He said he was only messing about, and she said she hoped there would be no repetition of the incident, or Scorpus would be in serious trouble.

So that might sound all right, but outside the classroom Scorpus had looked at us and said, in a low, fierce voice like he was acting the part of a baddie in a soap, 'I told you two losers if you told on me I'd kill you. And I *always* keep my word. See you after school.'

Our last class was History with Miss Spiggins, which was close to the main entrance, so we were able to get out of school fast and run all the way home before Scorpus appeared. So, OK, that was a result. But we couldn't keep dodging him for ever.

It turned out we'd picked the absolute worst person in the school to get on the wrong side of. Really. It was like making an enemy of Doctor Doom or Darth Vader or someone. Scorpus was a terror. A legend. He was the hardest kid in school, and last year he'd been suspended for assaulting a teacher. His dad was a well-known local hard case. He'd just come out of prison after doing time for breaking a man's jaw in a pub and then breaking the nose of the copper who came to arrest him. So I didn't want my mum and dad going up to the school to complain and get a meeting with Scorpus's parents so they could tell them off in their posh voices using lots of long words. I had a feeling that wouldn't exactly help.

So when my dad got in from work that evening and asked me how it was, I told him it was fine too.

'They didn't eat you then?' said Ben, scratching his head.

'No, not yet,' I said.

My dad sat back in the armchair and sighed. 'I'm glad your first day at school went well, Sam. Wish I could say the same about my day at work.'

'Why?' my mum said. 'They didn't . . . ?'

'They did,' my dad said, in this deep kind of gravelly voice he uses when he's being dead serious. 'Roger Haggerston said the restructuring is going to take place next month. And my department is . . . vulnerable.'

Mum looked stricken. Money's always been a bit tight in our house. Not as tight as in Evan's, but still. Tightish. We're not one of those families that has a giant plasma telly or buys a new car or goes on long-haul holidays.

'What do you mean, vulnerable?'

'I mean vulnerable – you know what that means, don't you?'

Maeve stuck her head round the living-room door. She was just about to go out with her friends – she was wearing a short skirt and a tight top and about two kilos of make-up, but she still looked incredibly bad-tempered. 'What? What's vulnerable?'

'My job.'

'What do you mean, Dad? They're giving you the *sack*?'

'It's not definite yet.'

'Oh great, that's *all* I need,' said Maeve, and flounced out, banging the front door behind her.

'I'll smash Roger Haggerston's face in!' Ben said. He's only six and it often looks like he's in a world of his own, but he picks everything up.

My mum's like, 'What are we going to *do*?'

'I don't know,' my dad said heavily. 'If the worst comes to the worst there'll be some redundancy money, but I don't know how much.'

'How can they do this to you, after sixteen years?'

'They can do what they want.'

He sounded so sad and weary that even the dog noticed, went up to my dad and stuck his head on his knee. Dad stroked the dog's ears.

'Come on, Billiam. Shall I take you for a walk?'

Billiam started leaping and capering about. My dad got up and went to get the lead.

'I'll come,' I said.

I just felt like getting out of the house. And maybe cheering my dad up a bit.

It turned out to be a fantastically good job I went.

It was just getting dark. Me and Dad walked along, not saying much. I was thinking about having to go to school tomorrow and I s'pose Dad was thinking about not having to go to work any more. But it was kind of comforting, somehow, to walk along together in silence.

A few streets from our house there's a bit of forest where you can let dogs off the lead. Billiam ran backwards and forwards, looking for a stick. He found one and dropped it at my feet. I threw it and he galloped off after it.

'So,' said Dad, 'tell me a bit more about school.'

'It was all right.'

'What lessons did you have?'

'Oh, you know. English and stuff. The usual.'

'You're Mr Communicative, aren't you? Did you make any new friends?'

'Well, not yet, I just went around with Evan.'

'But do they seem nice there? It's a good atmosphere?'

'Oh yeah, yeah. Very good. Yeah.'

I'd already decided I wasn't going to lay the Scorpus problem on him, but after hearing about him probably losing his job I wasn't going to even more. I didn't want to add to his worries.

Billiam came bounding back with the stick. I threw it again and he galloped off after it again.

Dad pointed upwards. 'Look!'

A bright silver streak was moving across the velvety blue sky.

'Is that a shooting star?'

'That's right.'

'You can make a wish on it?'

Dad laughed. 'Well, that's the story. It's really just a meteor, burning up as it hits the Earth's atmosphere. A chunk of rock from space. So I don't quite see how it could grant wishes . . .'

'Well, I'm going to wish,' I said. 'You never know!'

'Better hurry then, before it burns up!'

My mind started working fast. As fast as the meteor. I could wish that Scorpus would leave me and Evan alone. Or that I was so strong I could pick him up and chuck him over the school wall. But then, what about Dad and his job – maybe I should wish he'd keep it? Or even get a promotion? And then I thought, if I wished for a million pounds it wouldn't matter about his job. And it was *then* I thought, *What if I wished for a million wishes? Then I could take care of everything.*

I want to make it clear that I didn't actually *believe* in the wish at this point. I didn't really think a piece of hurtling space-rock could or would change the world for me. It was just comforting to think about it – like it's sort of comforting to pray sometimes, even if you don't believe in God.

So I said, in my head, *I wish for a million wishes.*

The shooting star disappeared behind the trees.

My dad's like, 'Did you wish?'

'Yeah, I wished.'

'What for?'

'Better not tell. Or it won't come true.'

My dad gave a little smile. A sort of slightly weary, grown-up smile. 'I don't expect it'll come true anyway, Sam.'

'No, I s'pose it won't.'

But in my head I was saying, *I wish Scorpus doesn't beat me or Evan up tomorrow. And I wish Dad keeps his job.*

Which meant, theoretically, I had nine hundred and ninety-nine thousand nine hundred and ninety-eight wishes left.

I didn't bother to wish for the million pounds, though. That seemed a bit *too* unlikely.

We turned back and went home, and I went to bed.

The alarm clock went off like a bomb, bursting through an uneasy dream I'd been having about running through the school corridors being chased by Scorpus, and I kept slamming doors behind me hoping to get at least two closed doors between me and him, but every time he flung open the previous door before I could shut the next one, if you see what I mean.

In books and films people always sit bolt upright in bed when they wake from a bad dream, but of course no one ever does that in real life. What you do is what I did – just lie there, feeling relieved it was only a dream, waiting for your heartbeat to slow down. Except in this case, I realized, there wasn't much to feel relieved about. The reality was as bad as the dream.

'Sam! Are you up yet?'

My mum's voice came floating up the stairs.

The clock said seven thirty. There was a parallelogram-shaped patch of sunlight on the wall at the end of my bed.

'Sam! Time to get up!'

I wish it was an hour earlier, I thought.

And that's when things got seriously weird.

My mum's voice stopped instantly. The clock said six thirty. And the patch of sunlight wasn't at the end of my bed, but at the corner of the room. And it wasn't a parallelogram any more. It was more like a rhombus.

This time I *did* sit up. Not bolt upright, but I struggled into a sitting position and clutched my head. Maybe I was still dreaming? But it didn't feel like it. Everything felt *real*. I felt the softness of the duvet, and the mattress shifting under me, heard birds singing outside and a car driving past in the distance.

This wasn't possible.

Was it?

'I wish I had . . . a cup of tea,' I said.

And a nanosecond later, there it was, gently steaming on my bedside table. In my favourite mug too, a blue one that I call 'Bluey'. (Yeah, very original, I know.) I took a sip. It was perfect. Just strong enough, with the right amount of milk, and one (level) spoonful of sugar.

It was so weird I wanted to burst out laughing. Could I get *anything* I wished for?

I wish I had scrambled egg on toast, with grilled bacon and a glass of orange juice. On a tray.

And the tray materialized, neatly balanced on my lap.

The food smelt delicious. I took a few mouthfuls, and it tasted delicious too. But I was too excited to finish it. I wanted to try out more wishes.

I wish I had a million pounds!

The whole lower end of my bed dipped, and I was bounced upwards, like on a see-saw, as a great big purple block of twenty-pound notes landed on it. It was about the size of a really big suitcase. *So that's what a million pounds looks like,* I thought.

I reached out and took one of the notes. It was brand new, as flat and crisp as if someone had ironed it. And I could have as many of these as I wanted . . .

But I'd have to be careful. Because the wishes came true as soon as I thought them. And thoughts are so difficult to control. They just pop into your head. As soon as you decide not to think something, you're already thinking it. So if I just happened to think, I don't know, *I wish there was a tiger in the room . . .*

No!

Too late.

There it was.

A massive orange-and-black beast, filling the space between my bed and the door, filling the room with its hot, wild, heavy, dangerous big-cat-smell. The floorboards creaked and strained under its weight. Its great big furry yellow-eyed face stared into mine. It looked startled, obviously wondering what had happened – one second it was hunting in the jungle in India or somewhere and the next it was in this little carpeted room on the first floor of a house in England. It swished its tail. It growled.

I could *feel* its strength – it could knock my head off with one swipe of a paw.

'I wish you were gone!' I said as fast as I could.

Blip.

Gone. Only the smell lingered.

So I wished for that to go too. And it did.

But I still had a problem. Any moment now another crazy thought could come into my head – like . . . *I wish—*

No, I don't—

I don't wish—

I wish the—

No, no, no, la-la-la-la, I don't wish that at all, no let's think of something else—

I wish the world—

No, no, focus on something else, like if the Incredible Hulk and the Mighty Thor had a fight, who'd—

I wish the world would—

No I don't stop stop stop no—

I wish the world would e—

No I don't – I –

– and I suddenly shouted, 'I wish my wishes would only come true when I say them aloud!'

I breathed out a long, shaky breath.

I'd come within a micro-second of wishing the world would end.

But now I was safe. I wasn't going to wish for anything stupid *aloud*, was I? To calm my jangled nerves, I wished for a little tiny orchestra to appear on top of the million-pound pile of twenties and play me some soothing music. And they appeared immediately, musicians the size of Action Men and Barbie dolls, the men in black suits, the women in long gowns and the conductor in tails and a white bow tie, and they started tuning up.

And I lay back, thinking of all the things I could wish for, but not doing anything about it yet, just luxuriating in the possibilities like a bubble bath. All my life, you see, ever since I was a really little kid, I've always wanted something magical to happen. When Mum used to read me stories, about witches and elves and unicorns and stuff, or the Narnia books, or later when I read the Harry Potter books for myself, I used to think what a pity it was, what a shame, that none of that magic stuff was actually *true*. That life just went on in the same old boring way, with the Earth spinning round at a fixed rate and gravity doing its job 24-7, and nobody could fly or go invisible or transmogrify. But *now* – now *anything* was possible. The miniature orchestra played a beautiful miniature melody, all tiny and tinkly like it came out of a music box, and I lay there thinking of being able to make myself as small as them, or as big as a mountain, or to be able to breathe underwater and swim as fast as a shark, or travel to outer space on a rocket-powered bicycle . . . I couldn't stop grinning.

At seven thirty the alarm went off again. The parallelogram of sunlight was back on the wall at the end of my bed. I wished the musicians would go back to wherever they came from, and I wished the million quid was stashed in the suitcase on top of my wardrobe.

And then my mum shouted up the stairs. 'Sam! Are you up yet?'

I gazed at my face in the bathroom mirror as I was cleaning my teeth. I looked surprisingly normal. My eyes were bright and I kept smiling, but apart from that you'd have said this was the face of an ordinary eleven-year-old boy, with ginger hair and a few freckles. Not someone who could have anything in the world he wanted just by asking for it. And then I thought, *This is* true, *isn't it? I'm not just dreaming or insane?*

I wanted to ask the meteor, or whatever it was, that had given me the wishes. And then I realized I could make that happen any time I wanted.

'I wish . . .' I began, and then stopped. I was about to wish for the Wish-Answerer to appear, but I realized I didn't know how big meteors were. It might be too big to fit in the bathroom. It might be bigger than the house.

'I wish that you'd make yourself small, Mr Wish-Answerer, and come here so I can ask you a few questions.'

A chunk of rock, about the size of my head, materialized on the bathroom shelf in front of me. It was a sort of dark grey with reddish patches. Black smoke rose from it. I could feel the heat it gave out. It had two little thin legs and two little thin arms like twigs, and it had a sort of face that looked like it was made out of marks and bumps in the rock. It had a couple of dark hollows for eyes and a sticking-out bit in the middle that looked like a beak, and there was a sort of gash or fissure for its mouth.

'Er . . . pleased to meet you,' I said.

That was a totally stupid thing to say, I know, but I was in a state of shock.

The Meteor didn't say anything, but bent its skinny legs to make a little bow.

'So – who are you?'

The Meteor still didn't say anything, but spread its skinny arms and gave a little shrug.

'OK, I *wish* you'd tell me who you are.'

I'm afraid there is no intelligible answer I could give you, the Meteor said. It had a posh, precise voice like a newsreader's. Its mouth didn't move, though. *My name would take seven weeks to utter and would leave you none the wiser.*

'But can you tell me – this is all true, isn't it? I'm not mad or dreaming?'

You are not mad and you are not dreaming, the Meteor confirmed.

'So – you've given me a million wishes, right? And I can really have anything I want?'

As long as it is logically possible.

'What do you mean?'

I cannot grant wishes that do not make logical sense. If you wished for a round square, for example, that wish could not be granted. Because no square by definition could ever be round.

Well, that was OK. I didn't want a round square anyway. The last thing I needed.

'Apart from things like that, though – whatever I wish for, I get? And there are no catches?'

Catches?

'Well, I mean, do I have to use the wishes wisely or something? Or do I have to wish for good things?'

It's none of my business, the Meteor said. *Wish for whatever you like.*

I looked at the Meteor's little rocky face and it looked back at me. It sounds crazy, I know, but I couldn't think of any more questions to ask.

'Well, I suppose you can go back into space now.'

Thank you, I will.

'Wait – if there's anything else I need to know, can I just wish for you to come back?'

You do not need to summon me. If you wish to know something, I will answer.

'OK,' I said. 'Well . . . Bye, then.'

The next instant, there was nothing on the bathroom shelf except a pot full of toothbrushes, Dad's razor and can of shaving foam, Mum's aloe vera shower gel and about a hundred little jars and tubes of stuff that Maeve rubbed in or squirted on to various parts of her body.

Walking to school with Evan. It was a mild morning, warm and bright. The trees still had all their leaves but they were just beginning to be tinged with yellow. I felt happier and more alive than I'd ever felt in my life.

I could turn the sky green if I wanted, I thought. *I could make the lamp posts dance.*

'What we gonna do?' said Evan. 'About Scorpus.'

'Don't worry, I'll sort him out.'

'What? How are you gonna do that?'

'I haven't decided yet.'

'Oh, that's great!' said Evan. 'He hasn't decided yet! Well, let me know when you come up with a plan, won't you? It is, you know, like slightly kind of urgent.'

'Don't worry.' And then I started whistling, which must've been kind of annoying, I know, especially as I can't really whistle.

Evan's like, 'Stop that horrible noise.'

He had a point. It was a bit tuneless and breathy, and I couldn't hit the high notes properly. Or the low ones either, really. So I said, 'I wish I could whistle really well,' and the next second a beautiful, rich melody came flowing out of me as if I was a blackbird or something. It was the same tune the mini orchestra had played. Dunno what it was, but it was nice.

Evan stared at me. 'You're weird this morning.'

'Am I? I tell you what, Evan, do you wish your uniform fitted you better?'

'Look, don't start—'

''Cause I do. I wish it fitted you perfectly.'

Evan's uniform moved on his body like it was a live thing. The sleeves flowed down to his wrists, the trouser-legs flowed down to his ankles and the jacket widened just the right amount.

Evan's mouth widened too. It looked like the Blackwall Tunnel.

'How – how did . . . ?'

'Magic.'

'No, but really – how?'

'Magic.'

'But what did you *do*?'

'Magic.'

That was all I'd answer, all the rest of the way to school. I guess it must have been kind of annoying.

CHAPTER THREE

All morning I was waiting for Scorpus to make his move, but somehow or other our paths didn't seem to cross. Obviously I could've just wished he'd come and find me, but I didn't quite want to do that. It didn't seem *sporting*, somehow, if you know what I mean. I wanted it to happen, like, naturally.

Anyway, the morning's lessons were fun, because they were so easy. Like in French – I'd never done French before, except for learning *Frère Jacques* in primary school, but I wished I spoke it perfectly, and astonished Miss Gravely by asking her, in perfect

French, where she'd spent her summer holiday and if she'd enjoyed it and was it the first time she'd been to Greece, and what did she think of the economic situation there, and did she agree that very hot weather was nice provided it wasn't too humid? Evan and the whole class just sort of goggled at me.

'How did you learn to speak French like that?' Evan said.

'Magic.'

It wasn't till lunchtime that Scorpus tracked us down. I was in the locker rooms with Evan, playing Wild Animals Top Trumps, but it wasn't much of a contest because I'd wished I knew what all his cards were. I'd just beaten his alligator (20 m.p.h.) with my hare (45 m.p.h.) when Vanida Mookjai came running in and squealed, 'Quick! Run! Scorpus is on his way!'

'Oh good,' I said. 'I've been wondering when he'd show up.'

'Let's get out of here!' said Evan.

'If you leave now,' I said, 'you'll miss all the fun.'

Anyway, there wasn't time to go anywhere, because the next moment Scorpus came and stood in the doorway of the locker room, with his long shadow streaming ahead of him, all the way to the tips of my toes. Two of his mates stood behind him. And there were more kids crowding behind them, keen to see the entertainment.

'Farter! Bogbrush! You're dead.'

I just laughed.

As Scorpus walked towards me, I muttered under my breath, 'I wish I was as strong as the Incredible Hulk, I mean as strong as he would be if he existed in real life.'

Immediately I felt a kind of awesome power flood my body. Like when you get an adrenalin rush, but twenty times more powerful. I felt like a volcano waiting to blow.

Scorpus reached out to grab me.

I smashed my fist into his body as hard as I could. I have to say the result wasn't *exactly* what I'd expected.

In the comics or the movies, when the Hulk hits someone they might get knocked through a wall or sent flying into the distance. But they always get up again. They don't have to go to hospital, they don't have broken bones, they don't *bleed*. But then, the Hulk normally hits enemies who have super-powers themselves. Or special armour or something.

This was different.

As my fist crashed into Scorpus's body there was a horrible splintering noise. He was catapulted back-wards and hit the wall with a thud, and he slid down so he was sitting on the floor with his head hanging on to his chest in a kind of grotesque manner. He couldn't seem to breathe, he was sort of heaving and moaning. Then he keeled over sideways and lay on the floor, completely still.

Oh terrific.

There was a horrified hush and then everyone who was watching started babbling at once.

'My God!'

'Oh my *God*!'

'Did you see that?'

'He just—'

'*Oh* my *God*!'

'Never seen anything like it!'

'Is he dead?'

'What did you *do*, man?' said Evan.

'I don't know.' Then, under my breath, I said, 'I wish I knew what's wrong with Scorpus.'

And the posh, solemn newsreader's voice of the

Meteor, inside my head, went: *He has a fractured sternum, seven cracked ribs and a punctured lung.*

Oh.

Right.

Just a *bit* more severe than I'd intended.

'OK,' I said quietly, 'I wish Scorpus didn't have a fractured sternum and cracked ribs and a punctured lung. I wish he'd stop bleeding. I wish he'd get up.'

Scorpus sort of hauled himself to his feet. He stood there in a kind of tottery way, and what with his pale face and the blood still trickling down his chin he looked like a zombie in a horror movie.

I put on this cold, hard voice like a teacher telling someone off – like Mrs Protheroe should have told Scorpus off, but she wasn't really strict enough. 'Scorpus, if there is any repetition of your thuggish behaviour you'll be in serious trouble. You'll wish you'd never been born, Scorpus. I'll come down on you like a ton of bricks.' (That was one of my dad's expressions.) 'Do you get me?'

Scorpus just stared at me in what you might call a dazed manner.

'I *said,* do you *get* me?'

Scorpus slowly nodded.

'Then I suggest you go away and think very hard about what you've done and what it's led to. I think there are some lessons there for you, if you think about it very carefully.'

Scorpus staggered away. The crowd parted to let him through.

I suddenly realized I was drenched in sweat. And my heart was hammering away like, well, like a hammer. In the hands of a demented hammerer.

I wished I wasn't as strong as the Hulk any more, in case I hurt someone by accident.

But I felt good. Oh man, I felt ... brilliant.

CHAPTER FOUR

alking home with Evan.

'All right,' Evan demanded. 'What's happening?'

'How do you mean?'

'You know what I mean! Are you really . . . *magic*?'

I thought about this. 'Yeah, I s'pose you could say that.'

'But – *how* . . . ?'

'I wished upon this shooting star, I wished for a million wishes, and—'

'Wait a minute,' Evan said. 'That's not possible. A shooting star is just—'

'I know, it's just a meteor. A chunk of space-rock.'

'So how can it grant wishes?'

'I dunno. It just did, that's all.'

'But . . .' Evan went quiet and a sort of lost-in-thought look appeared on his face. He does this look sometimes. It's like he's gazing off into the remote distance trying to make out something no one else can see, and he ignores everything else.

'What?'

'Can you prove it?'

'What do you want me to do?'

'Wish for . . . an ice cream.'

To be honest I was a bit disappointed in Evan. I thought he might have come up with something more interesting than that. But then he is a bit of a greedy pig, so it's not that surprising I s'pose.

'Sure thing. What flavour?'

'Vanilla and chocolate. Double scoop.'

'Cone or tub?'

'Cone.'

'Do you want anything on it?'

'Er, yeah, nuts and chocolate sauce.'

'Did you get all that, Wish-Answerer? I wish for a double scoop of vanilla and chocolate ice cream, in a cone, nuts and chocolate sauce. Actually, make it two.' I quite fancied one myself.

The two ice creams materialized, one in each of my hands, so suddenly it made me jump. I offered one to Evan.

Evan took it warily and peered at it as if it might hold some kind of explanation.

I licked mine. It was nice. 'Go on, try it.'

Evan licked his. 'It's . . . *real*. It's . . . *delicious*.'

'Oh, yes, you only get good stuff with my wishes.'

'But – I just don't get where they came from. Stuff can't appear out of nothing!'

'It can with my wishes.'

'But – *how*?'

'It's no good asking how, that's just the way they work. It's like – the laws of the universe. Gravity. That just works, doesn't it, and no one knows how?'

'But that's my point! You've just *broken* the laws of the universe. You can't make ice cream and chocolate and nuts out of . . . *air*. Things just work in a certain way, they always have done. One element doesn't change into another, just 'cause someone says they wish it would! Gravity always operates in the same way. Water never flows uphill. Light always travels at the same speed. All that stuff. Those laws never change.'

'Never up until *now*,' I said. 'But things are different now I've got my wishes!'

Evan put on his lost-in-thought look again. 'Look, if you're saying that you can just change the laws of physics whenever you like . . . That's kind of . . . hard to accept. Without a *lot* of evidence. Could you do, like, an experiment to prove it?'

'Sure thing. Like what?'

'Well then – *can* you make water flow uphill?'

'Easy-peasy lemon-squeezy!' I said. 'I wish for a bottle of water.' It appeared in my hand. 'Now, watch this.'

The road we were standing on was a hill – not a steep one, but enough so that if you rode a bike up it, it was harder work than you expected – I knew from experience. I spilt the water on the ground, and of course it immediately started to run down the hill, following all the little cracks in the pavement.

'I wish you'd start running uphill, water!' I told it.

The water collected itself and then started to crawl uphill, like a glistening, silvery snake. We watched it get smaller and smaller as it crawled away from us.

Then Evan looked at me.

I looked at Evan.

And we both burst out laughing.

There didn't seem to be anything else to do.

When we stopped laughing, I said, 'What shall we wish for now then? Anything you like, just tell me.'

Evan looked thoughtful again. He looked as if he was about to speak, then stopped.

'What?'

'No, nothing, I'll leave it to you. They're your wishes. You choose.'

He looked at me expectantly, and I got a feeling there was something he wanted me to say, but I had no idea what it was.

'I tell you what,' I said. 'You were talking yesterday about *Gulliver's Travels*. Wouldn't it be fun to go really giant, so everyone was tiny . . . ?'

'Er, yeah,' Evan said. Then he seemed to get more interested in the idea. 'Yeah, that would be really great!'

'Let's do it!' I said. A strange excitement started to prickle in my belly. 'We'd better go somewhere with a bit more space, though. Otherwise we'll be tripping over houses and stepping on cars and stuff.'

'We could walk up to the Common.'

'Walk?' I said. 'No need to bother with *that*!' And it occurred to me then that I wouldn't need to walk anywhere ever again, if I didn't want to. Not that I've got anything against walking, in fact sometimes I quite like it, but it's a bit, you know, time-consuming. 'I wish we were up at the Common.'

So the next instant there we were. The sudden change took my breath away. Green space all around us. A pleasant breeze blowing. There were a few dog-walkers dotted about, and on the far side some little kids and their parents in the playground, and about a hundred metres away some boys were having a kick-about. They were going to get the shock of their lives in a minute, I thought.

'How big do you want to go?' I said.

'I dunno – about twenty metres high?'

'Sounds about right to start with. 'Course, we can always go bigger if we want to.'

''Course we can.'

My heart was pumping away like a crazer and my stomach was doing cartwheels. I couldn't quite believe what we were about to do.

'Ready?'

'Ready.'

'We'd better stand a bit further apart,' I said. 'Otherwise when we start to grow we'll bump into each other.'

'Oh, yeah.' He moved off, about fifteen metres away.

'Ready?'

'Wait – I just thought of something. You better wish our clothes grow too, or we'll burst out of them and be naked. And that'll be embarrassing.'

'OK. I wish me and Evan were giants, twenty metres high, and our clothes still fitted us, and we were all in the same proportions as now.' I didn't want to be like a great long skinny piece of string, I wanted to be an actual giant, like in fairy tales.

And so . . . we started to grow.

It was the weirdest feeling. I could see the ground getting further and further away, as if I was going up in a lift or a cable car, but at the same time I could feel the ground sort of expanding under the soles of my growing feet. And I could see Evan swelling up beside me, an idiotic grin of excitement on his face. We were inflating like a couple of giant balloons.

Only – this was the weirdest thing of all – we weren't getting lighter, like a balloon would as it filled up with air. We were getting *heavier*. I could feel my head drooping on my neck, like my neck was too feeble to hold it up properly. And my body was getting so massive my legs couldn't support it properly. Even though my legs were growing too, they weren't up to the job of keeping me upright, I was just *too* heavy. They started to buckle, I could feel them giving at the knees. I tried to wave my arms to help me keep my balance, but they were almost too heavy to move, it was like trying to wave tree trunks around.

I was going to fall, and I knew that falling from this height, at this weight, would be serious. I mean, *really* serious.

I mean, like, fatal.

I saw my own expression of panic mirrored on Evan's face as he tottered helplessly around.

'Quick!' His voice had gone deep and booming. 'Wish we were lighter than air, or we're goners!'

'I wish we were lighter than air!'

Oh, the relief! The sweet merciful life-saving

relief as I floated up off the ground! The horrible weight of my head that felt like it was going to break my neck was gone, my limbs were light and free, and the ground was no longer a terrifying enemy that was about to kill me, but a nice wide stretch of green grass that looked peaceful and friendly as I gradually rose above it.

The people on the Common were all pointing up and staring, shouting and jabbering, unable to believe their eyes.

'Whew!' Evan said. He was hovering just a few metres away. 'That was close!'

'What happened?' I couldn't figure it out. 'Why did we get so heavy? I didn't wish for that!'

Evan's like, 'I should have thought of it. Of course when you get bigger you get heavier!'

'Yeah, obviously, but I still don't get it. If we're bigger all over—'

'That's the problem. The thing is, we got bigger in three dimensions. So we're over ten times *taller* than before, but more than a thousand times *heavier*.'

'But what about dinosaurs? They were giant, and they could walk about OK.'

'Yeah, but they'd evolved to be like that. Their

skeletons were built to hold their weight. We're not the right *shape* to be so big, we weren't designed for it.'

All this time we'd been drifting upwards. Already the ground was far away. The Common now looked like a green spot in the middle of a big grey town. People looked like ants and cars were like little beetles. And it was getting cold. Like, really cold. What my dad would call brass monkeys weather.

'It's freezing!' My teeth were chattering. And you can imagine the racket that made, when each tooth was about the size of an iPad.

'We're gonna keep rising 'cause we're lighter than air!' His teeth were going like a set of giant castanets as well. 'And it's gonna get colder and colder and soon we won't be able to breathe. You have to do something!'

'OK, OK, I get it!' I thought for a second. 'Right, I wish we were heavier than air, but only a bit heavier. I want us to be able to walk around OK. And also I wish we don't tread on anyone or squash anyone, all right?'

We started to sink, quite fast, but not scarily fast. It was like dangling from a parachute. Or that's what I'd guess, anyway, seeing as I've never done a parachute jump. The air got warmer again. My giant goosebumps disappeared.

The green grass came surging towards us. There were more people there now, hundreds of them, all around the edges of the Common, and there were cops trying to keep them back. They all had their phones out, taking pictures of us. A TV camera crew was just arriving, piling out of their vans and setting up equipment.

'I've always wanted to be on the telly!' I said.

Evan grinned and was just saying 'Me too!' when we landed. It made us stagger a bit, and we both lurched towards the watching crowds. They screamed and starting to stampede backwards, falling over and treading on each other. It was crazy.

Oh great, I thought. I said, 'I wish no one gets hurt, and I wish no one was scared of us.'

The crowd calmed down then. They regrouped and pressed nearer to us, craning their necks up and going 'Wow!', 'Ooh!', 'Aah!' etc, etc, like people do when they're watching really amazing fireworks or something.

'What shall we do now?' I said.

'Go for a walk?' Evan suggested.

'Yeah, why not?'

So we walked off the Common and into the town. It was weird 'cause each step bounced us up in the air and then we came drifting down again. It was like walking on the moon.

The crowd followed us, and more people joined them as we bounced along through the streets. They were running out of their houses, pouring down the streets towards us from every direction.

It was funny seeing the town from this height. Houses came just past our knees, and even blocks of flats were only around head height. And I could see all the different roads and streets and the way they were laid out – for the first time I really got the shape and pattern of the town I'd lived in all my life. It was a bit like when I went on holiday to the Isle of Wight when I was eight, and we went to this place, Godshill, where they had a model village you could walk around. But this was a model village with real tiny people in it, running after us, or waving at us from top-floor windows.

Well, you might think you'd never get bored of being a giant and walking around being followed by cheering crowds and filmed by TV crews (a couple of helicopters had turned up and they had cameras going too). But the truth is, once we'd walked round town a couple of times the novelty started to wear off. I mean, it was still great, but I started to think, *What next?*

'What next?' Evan said.

'I dunno. Do you want to go even bigger?'

'I dunno.'

I heard a tiny voice squeaking 'Sam! Sam!' and I looked down and there was Maeve with three of her friends in the High Street.

I bent down. 'Hiya Maeve.'

'Sam! What's happened?' Her eyes were bright with amazement and she was grinning her head off. I realized it was the first time I'd seen her so excited or interested in anything for ages. She'd been in a bad mood ever since her boyfriend, Stefan Bumgarner, dumped her. (That's not a joke, by the way. He really is called that.) He'd started going out with another girl who Maeve really hates, Josephine Waxwing. And she'd hardly smiled since. She must have been feeling pretty depressed, I s'pose.

'How did you get so *big*?' she squealed.

'Growth spurt, I guess.' I put my hand flat on the pavement in front of her. 'Climb on, I'll show you the view from up here!'

They all scrambled up and squashed together on my hand – which to them was about the size of a double bed. I slowly rose up, holding my hand as steady as I could. They were all screaming with laughter and clutching on to each other and sliding about.

It was when they were about ten metres up that the accident happened.

Loren stumbled and caught hold of Lola who also stumbled and they tripped over my thumb – so to save them I tilted my hand – but I tilted it too far and too quickly, and Maeve and Miriam slid off the other side and went plummeting down, screaming their heads off.

I made a desparate grab at them with my free hand, but missed. They hit the pavement with two sickening cracks, like a pair of eggs being dropped.

The crowd gasped.

'Whoops!' said Evan.

Maeve and Miriam lay sprawled out, limbs twisted, unmoving.

The helicopters swept down towards the bodies to get better pictures.

A feeling of guilt and dread filled me, as if I'd just smashed two priceless vases in a museum or something, only much, much worse because they weren't things, they were *people,* and one of them was my own sister. I'd only had the wishes a few hours and already I'd seriously injured or killed three people. I was like a one-man crime wave.

But I still had the wishes, didn't I? That was the great thing about having a million wishes (or nine hundred and ninety-nine thousand nine hundred and whatever-it-was). Nothing was unchangeable. Consequences were optional.

'I wish they were alive again,' I said. 'And completely unhurt.'

Maeve and Miriam got up, dusting themselves off. The crowd sighed with relief.

'Sam, you stupid idiot!' Maeve shouted up at me.

'Sorry, bit of a butterfingers there . . .' That's one of my mum's expressions. It seemed to fit.

'You could have killed us!'

'Yeah, well, I didn't.'

I put the other two girls down beside Maeve and

Miriam. Carefully.

One of the helicopters buzzed right in front of my head and I could see the cameraman training his camera on me, trying to get a good shot of my face. I had to fight off an urge to swat it away like a fly. Now the whole stupid episode of me dropping those girls would be on the news, it would be broadcast by TV companies all over the world and get a billion hits on YouTube . . .

I looked at Evan and he gave me a look with raised eyebrows and a downturned mouth, shrugging his shoulders, and I realized I was doing the same look myself, and the look meant, 'What the heck are we doing here?' Suddenly the idea of being on telly didn't seem so brilliant, and stomping round the streets of town while being twenty metres tall didn't seem big or clever any more. Well, it was big, obviously, but not clever.

I'm like, 'Let's get out of this.'

Evan nodded his colossal head.

I'm like, 'I wish me and Evan were normal size again.' And immediately, *so* immediately it made me feel giddy, we were standing on the pavement together, normal size like everyone else, and trees and buildings we'd looked down on a moment ago now towered over us. 'And I wish those helicopters would buzz off. I wish everyone would just forget seeing us as giants. I wish the film in all the camera crews' cameras turns out to be blank.'

The crowd lost interest in what you might call an abrupt manner. They streamed off in different directions. Maeve and her friends went off towards the shopping centre without another glance at us.

'Now what?' Evan said.

'I dunno,' I said. 'Tell you what – we've tried being giants. How about being tiny next? Just like Gulliver. That'd be a laugh.'

'Yeah, I s'pose it would.'

I'd always been fascinated by the idea of being really teeny-tiny, so that ordinary objects were giant-sized – you know, like a pencil would be the size of a telegraph pole and a pea would be like a pumpkin and a caterpillar would be like a giant snake with legs.

But I didn't want to go small here in the High Street. I didn't want to draw attention to ourselves again, which would definitely happen if we suddenly disappeared. Also, we might get trodden on. Better to do this one indoors, at least to start with.

'Let's go to my house first.'

'All right.' He turned to start walking off.

'What you doing? Walking's a thing of the past, man!'

'Oh yeah. Right.'

'I wish me and Evan were in my bedroom.'

My bedroom walls appeared around us, and the bed materialized so suddenly behind me that I sat down on it.

CHAPTER FIVE

 ow small do you wanna go?'

Evan considered this. 'About ten centimetres? For starters?'

'You got it. I wish we were ten centi-metres tall, and our clothes still fitted!'

The room seemed to explode. The walls went rushing away and the ceiling zoomed upwards. My wardrobe on the other side of the room suddenly looked like a block of flats. The bed I was sitting on turned into a massive great area, about the size of a five-a-side football pitch. A soft, bouncy five-a-side football pitch.

Evan was on the carpet, looking up at me. The drop from my bed to the floor was about half a metre, I guess, but at my current size that was equivalent to about seven and a half metres. It made me feel dizzy.

'How do I get down from here?'

'Can't you climb?'

It was true that there was a bit of duvet hanging over the edge. If I climbed down that and dangled from the end, I'd be near enough the ground to be able to drop the last bit. Still, it looked pretty scary. If I slipped . . .

'Or you could just wish to be down here,' Evan said.

Well, that was true too. But I suddenly thought, what's the point of always wishing things were already done, instead of doing them? Being tiny was an adventure, after all – I might as well make the most of it.

I grabbed the duvet and started to inch down. It was harder than I'd thought. Gripping a fistful of duvet is easy when you're full-sized. But at ten centimetres high, your hands are so small they can't grab very much of it. It felt much coarser than normal, like stiff sacking.

I started to sweat. I glanced down and the ground still looked a long, long way away. If I fell I'd be all smashed up, like when Maeve fell off my hand earlier . . .

And then I felt my hands slipping.

I fell, leaving my stomach behind.

The wind rushed past my ears.

I heard Evan give a sort of squeak of alarm.

Too late, I started to shout 'I wish—'

I hit the floor.

But I didn't hit it with a bang. It was more a sort of *ploomph*, plus a little bit of a rustle. It didn't hurt at all. The carpet was deep and springy, coming up to my ankles.

'Are you all right?' Evan ran towards me over the springy carpet.

'Totally. It feels like I just fell, well, off a bed.'

Evan laughed. 'Of *course*! You *did* just fall off a bed. It looks a long way to us, but it's still only a short drop really – and because we weigh so much less, you hit with much less force than usual. Do you realize what this means?'

'No – what?'

'We don't have to worry about gravity at all. At this size, it can't hurt us! Watch!'

He ran across the room and started trying to climb up the wardrobe, but it was too smooth and he kept slipping down.

'Wish I was on top of the wardrobe, Sam!'

'OK, I wish you were on top of the wardrobe.'

There he was, next to my suitcase full of money. I'd forgotten about that. He spread his arms like a diver and launched himself off into space.

I clutched my face in alarm – even though he'd said it was safe it did still look like a horribly long drop...

He hit the carpet, rolled and got up grinning all over his face.

'You try!'

So for the next five minutes we played at jumping off the wardrobe. It was amazing – like bungee jumping, I guess, but we didn't have to worry about hitting the ground. We were so light we *couldn't* hurt ourselves.

'I bet we could jump from higher – I bet we could jump from the roof of the house!'

I'm like, 'D'you reckon?'

"Course. Look, we only weigh about as much as mice – and if a mouse fell off the roof it would be OK, wouldn't it?'

'I dunno.'

'Wish you knew, then.'

'Oh yeah. I wish I knew if a mouse would hurt itself if it fell off the roof of our house.'

And the little newsreader's voice in my head said, *No. It would receive a slight shock and scamper away unharmed.*

'I wish we were on the roof of our house, then!'

We sat on the ridge at the very top of the roof. Slate-grey tiles, each one about the size of our bathroom floor, sloped away from us. The garden was so far below it looked like another country.

'This is it,' Evan said. 'The big one!'

I took a deep breath.

Evan stood up. 'You ready?'

I nodded. I stood up.

I heard a beat of wings behind me and a massive great bird swooped down and snatched me up in its horrible, big, spiky talons, and flew off with me.

CHAPTER SIX

he talons were gripping me tightly and it really hurt. I craned my neck round to look at the bird. It was like something out of a horror film. When you see birds pecking about on the lawn they can look quite cute. But when you see them really close-up they're about as cute as a great white shark. This one had a cruel, curved beak and blank, psychotic eyes. It was planning to eat me, and it wouldn't suffer a moment's remorse. Scientists say birds are descended from dinosaurs, and all I can say is, I believe it.

'I wish I was my normal size again!'

The bird gave a squawk of surprise. Its talons slipped off me. And I started to fall at accelerating speed to earth, which, now I was normal-sized again, was capable of killing me. I was also completely naked, as I'd forgotten to wish my clothes would grow with me.

'I wish I was ten centimetres again!' I got the wish out just before I hit the lawn. So I didn't do myself any serious damage, but it was an uncomfortable landing. Now I was tiny again, each blade of grass was about thigh-high, and as thick as my hand. It also felt very hard and coarse – more like reeds than grass.

This was turning out to be a stressful day.

I wished for my clothes back. I also wished that the bird would have a really bad headache for the rest of the day. A bit spiteful, maybe. But after all, that was nothing compared to what it would've done to me.

Evan had watched all this from the roof, and now he jumped down beside me on the lawn.

'Wow, that was close!'

'Tell me about it.'

'That was a sparrowhawk! They're quite rare round here, you know.'

'They can't be too rare for me.'

'But you have to admit, they're magnificent birds.'

'What?'

'They're magnificent birds.'

'You wouldn't say that if one had just carried you off.'

'Yes I would.'

'No you wouldn't.'

'Yes I would.'

'All right then, let's see. I wish a sparrowhawk would come along and carry Evan off.'

Down it swooped. Evan's face as he was carried off, dangling from its talons, featured three big circles – his round, astonished eyes and his round, gaping mouth.

It sounds mean, I know. It's just . . . when it's so easy to wish for something and you *know* it'll come true straight away, you often find yourself wishing for stuff before you've really thought it through.

In no time Evan was a speck in the distance. I wished the bird would bring him back unharmed and put him down on the ground beside me. So it came winging its way back, and as Evan came into focus I saw that now his face wasn't defined by three circles but by three straight lines. His eyes were narrowed and his lips were set in a line of crossness.

'Do you still think it's a magnificent bird, then?' I asked him.

'Yes, it's magnificent. But you're not!' His face was flushed and he was panting slightly. 'Look!' He pulled up his shirt to show big red weals where the talons had gripped him.

'All right then, I wish those red marks were gone.' At once Evan's skin was back to its pale, unmarked, flabby normality. 'Happy now?'

'Not really.'

'Well, what else can I do?'

'You could try saying sorry.'

Now, I don't know about you, but I hate being told to say sorry. I'm happy to say it if I *feel* sorry, but as soon as someone orders me to say it, I stop feeling it. So I really didn't want to say it. But then, I didn't want Evan to carry on feeling annoyed with me. So . . .

'I wish Evan didn't feel annoyed with me any more.'

'I don't,' Evan said. He grinned. 'I'm not annoyed with you at all.'

'Well, that's all right then. What shall we do now?'

'I'm getting a bit hungry,' said Evan.

What a surprise.

Still. I s'pose I was kind of peckish myself. 'What shall we have?'

'Burger and chips?'

'Coming right up. I wish for two Burger King Whoppers and fries . . .' Then my mind took a leap. 'Giant-sized!'

Wow.

I've always been fascinated by the idea of giant-sized food. And there it was, steaming, smelling delicious, two boxed burgers, each one about the size of a van. And next to each one, a bag as high as my head, with golden fries poking out of it like planks of wood.

I pulled one of the chips out. I had to use both hands. It was too hot to hold for long, so I wished for it to cool down, just a little bit, and then I took a bite.

Hmm.

It wasn't *quite* as delicious as I'd thought. For a start, the outside was a bit leathery – of course it was about fifteen times as thick as before, so quite hard to bite into. Also, when you're not much bigger than the chip yourself, you notice just how greasy they are. That is, very greasy indeed. And the fine dusting of salt they have, well, when you're ten centimetres tall it's not a fine dusting at all but chunks of rock salt, each one about as big as a grain of rice. I took a few bites all the same, but soon got tired of it and put the chip down in the grass. So did Evan.

'Perhaps the burgers will be better,' Evan said.

It was hard to wrestle the boxes open, so I just wished they'd open up. We each climbed into a box. The burger came up to about my waist, and by leaning forwards and spreading my arms I could just about touch both sides. I saw Evan was tearing chunks out of the bread and then pulling out fistfuls of burger to put in them – effectively making mini-burgers, which turned out to be the only way we could eat them. Even then it wasn't easy. We couldn't eat the sesame seeds, they were far too big and hard, so we had to pull those out and throw them away. The sauce and mayo and stuff inside, well, there was such a lot of it, buckets of it, and it got all over my clothes, adding to the grease stains the chip had already left there. The lettuce was thick and fibrous, like giant raw cabbage leaves. And the meat was coarse and gristly and fatty.

It *was* fun, because it was so weird. But it wasn't particularly nice to eat. Soon I felt sick and had to stop. Evan battled on gamely for a bit, but eventually even he had to give up.

We lay on the grass – I wished for a miniaturized patch so it would be more comfortable – and sipped on glasses of Coke I'd wished for – micro-sized, like us, otherwise the bubbles would have been too big to swallow.

And I tried to work out, in my head, what exactly having all these wishes meant and what I was going to do with them. I mean, so far, all I'd done was mess about. Was I going to carry on doing that? Well, maybe. It was pretty spectacular messing about, after all. But . . . it might get boring. No, not even boring, that wasn't the right word. More sort of . . . *unsatisfying*. Like just *playing* at life, instead of actually living it. Because when you can have whatever you want, without any effort at all – did anything actually mean anything?

'Sam?'

'Yeah?'

'You could wish for *anything*, couldn't you?'

'Looks that way.'

'No limits?'

'I don't think so.'

'Well . . . I wonder if . . . you could . . . ?'

'What?'

'I was just thinking . . .'

'What?'

'You know.' He looked at me with a kind of hopeful, pleading expression.

'What?' Maybe you'll think it was pretty dumb of me, but I couldn't work out what he was trying to lead up to.

Just then, a distraction occurred. 'Hey, look at that!' I said.

A line of ants was marching up the side of one of the burger boxes. And another line was heading for the discarded fry. But when I say ants, you have to realize that, from our perspective, these really were big, bad boys. Each one was roughly the size of a lobster.

'Oh my God!' said Evan. He wandered over to look at them more closely. So did I. They took no notice of us, just kept on filing past like robots. 'They're kind of horrible, aren't they?' Evan said.

'Like little monsters. Or aliens.'

'I wonder what they'd look like if we were *really* small?'

We looked at each other.

'I wish we were one millimetre tall!' I said, and the world changed.

The blades of grass were no longer reeds, but trees. They towered over our heads, casting a green gloom. The soil under our feet wasn't smooth but rough and chunky, full of clods and pebbles. And the ants – the ants! They were as big as rhinos now. You could actually hear the swoosh of the grass they parted, and hear their feet – if ants have feet. You know what I mean, the ends of their legs – grating on the pebbles as they tramped past.

In *Honey, I Shrunk the Kids*, if you've seen that film, the kids meet an ant in the garden and make friends with it. It's a cute ant and it communicates with them by squeaking and twitching its antennae, and it lets them ride around on its back. I have to tell you that that film is totally bogus. There's *nothing* cute about ants. They're cosmically ugly. When you see them close up in supersize it's amazing how crude and unfinished they look, like they're bolted together out of spare parts. They've got horrible, big goggly eyes which are completely empty of expression, and coarse hairs like steel wires sticking out of their legs, and great big mandibles dripping with some sort of horrible saliva. They've got a sort of pungent, acidic smell to them as well, like a mixture of sweat and vinegar. You can just tell, looking at them, that they have no soul, no intelligence whatsoever, they are just dumb machines blindly following a programme. Creepy or what? I felt a sudden, senseless desire to kill them. Destroy them all.

'Shall we?' I go.

'What?'

'Blast them.'

'But why?'

'It'll be fun.'

'But it's killing for fun, isn't it? Like hunting. And I don't agree with hunting.'

'Neither do I. But come on, Evan, these are *ants*! They haven't got any feelings. Look at them!'

'Well . . .'

I could see he was wavering. 'I wish we had a bazooka each, just the right size for us to hold but powerful enough to blow up an ant!'

And there, in my hands, was this sort of steel tube with a trigger and a telescopic sight. I lifted it on to my shoulder and looked down the sight at the nearest ant. I aimed at its bulky, bulbous head and pressed the trigger.

Wham!

A stream of yellow fire shot out and hit the ant. It burst into flames and fell over, with its six legs jerking about randomly.

A second later another streak of flame shot out from Evan's bazooka and another ant went up in flames and fell over.

The other ants took no notice. They just skirted round their fallen comrades and headed straight on for that burger. And I think it was this that convinced me that the ants deserved no mercy at all. They didn't even care about each other, so why should I?

I pumped the trigger again and again and again, and so did Evan, and the big lumbering brutes collapsed, burst into pieces, writhing and kicking, with no idea what had hit them. I realized I was laughing, and so was Evan.

It had been a dry summer. The flames from the

burning ants soon caught the surrounding grass. In no time a forest fire had started. Me and Evan retreated, still firing, but the flames were roaring towards us. I felt the heat searing my face.

'Sam!' Evan shouted. 'Do something!'

'I wish we were full-size!'

Blast. I'd forgotten about the clothes again. The doll-sized outfits we'd worn lay torn and tattered on the grass, and we were both stark naked.

'All right, I wish we had our clothes on, obviously!'

We stood on the lawn, with the little ring of fire flickering at our feet. The ants were running around in circles, tiny, confused black specks – the burger called them on while the flames drove them away.

I felt suddenly sorry for them. The poor little things didn't know what they were doing, they just followed their instincts. I started to stamp out the flames, and so did Evan. I tried to avoid stamping on any ants. But that was impossible, of course.

When the fire was out, I felt a bit silly and ashamed of myself. What had we just been doing? It was like we'd gone mad.

'I wish all those ants we'd killed were alive again,' I said.

Evan nodded in agreement. 'What's the matter with us? With all those wishes – you could do anything in the world – and we're wasting our time killing *ants*!'

'I know.'

'I mean, instead of killing things, we could . . .'

'What? Look, if there's something you want me to wish, why don't you just tell me?'

Evan bit his lip. 'You mean you can't guess?'

'Nothing's coming to me.'

'Well – have a think, OK?'

'OK.' He'd gone all serious. I couldn't work out why he was acting so weird.

'I'm gonna go home now,' Evan said.

'OK. See you tomorrow.'

At the garden gate he turned back. 'Just one more thing . . .'

'Yeah?'

'Could you wish for a burger for me to eat on the way home? A normal-sized one?'

'Sure,' I said. 'Was that it – the thing you wanted me to guess?'

'No,' Evan said. 'That wasn't it.'

CHAPTER SEVEN

 could tell by the way Dad came home that evening that he was in a good mood. He flung the door open and bounced into the hall. He was carrying a bottle of wine in one hand and a bunch of flowers in the other. And his face looked ... bright. Happy. Young.

Mum came out into the hall. He handed her the flowers and gave her a kiss.

'What's with the flowers? What have you done?'

'I've kept my job!'

'What? How come?'

'I don't know. Roger Haggerston came into my

office today and told me my job was guaranteed!'

'So they're not restructuring?'

'I don't know. But if they do, my job won't be affected!'

'That's great news, Dad!' I said.

Maeve appeared at the top of the stairs. She'd just got out of the bath and she was in a dressing gown with a towel wrapped round her head. 'What? You're not getting the sack?'

'No, Maeve. I'm not getting the sack.'

'That's something, I suppose.' She disappeared back into her room.

'But are you sure you can trust them?' Mum said suspiciously. She's found it hard to trust anyone since things all went wrong with her own job. She used to be the manager of an art shop. But she left because she wanted to be an artist herself. She spent every day painting in the shed at the end of the garden. But she never sold a single painting, even though the shop she used to manage let her put on an exhibition there. Then she tried to get her old job back but the owner had given it to someone else.

'Oh, I think so. Roger sounded like he meant it.'

'You might even get a promotion, Dad!' I said.

Dad laughed. 'Well, you never know.'

'That's right,' I said. 'You never know!'

'We should have a special dinner to celebrate!' Dad said.

Mum looked doubtful. 'Just because you've kept your job – for the time being – doesn't mean we have to spend your salary all at once. We still have to budget, you know.'

'Well, I know, but . . .'

I went into the kitchen, where no one could hear me, and made a few quick wishes.

A few moments later there was a knock at the door. I went back into the hall to watch Mum open it. There was a Chinese man standing there with two great big bags. A delicious smell of Chinese food wafted into the house.

'Madam, I am from Jade Garden, new gourmet Chinese restaurant, finest in area. As special promotion we bring you, honoured customers chosen at random, special Emperor's Banquet, entirely free of charge. Enjoy!'

He left the bags on the doorstep, got on his moped and zoomed off into the twilight.

Dad poked his nose into the bags and peeled back

the lid of one of the plastic containers. The smell of delicious food intensified.

'Is it some sort of joke?' my mum said.

'I don't think so,' Dad said. 'At least, the food seems real enough!'

Ben ran out of the living room. 'Is that Chinese?'

'Yeah,' I said, 'it's the Emperor's Banquet.'

'My flavourite!' said Ben. He said that by mistake years ago and everyone laughed, so he carried on saying it. We don't laugh any more, we're actually a bit fed up with it.

'Let's lay the table and open the wine!' my dad said. 'This is turning out to be a strange day. But a good one! I wonder what'll happen next?'

'I expect there'll be an earthquake and the house will fall down a chasm,' said my mum. 'Or we'll all be trapped in a fire.' She likes to bring things back down to earth.

'No, I think some other good stuff might happen,' I said. 'It's just a feeling I've got.'

While we were eating (it was the most delicious Chinese food any of us had ever eaten – I'd wished that it would be) the phone went. Mum went to get it.

We could hear her going, 'What? . . . Who is this? . . . Yes . . . But . . . Is this for real? . . . I can't quite believe this is happening, but . . .' Then she burst out laughing – not the sort of laugh when something's funny, but the sort of laugh when you're so happy you can't stop yourself. 'Of course! I'd be delighted! Yes . . . tomorrow . . . See you then, I can't wait!'

She came back to the table. Her face was pink and dazed with delight.

'What is it, Mum?' Maeve goes.

'That was Bernard Souter! The art critic, you know. He said . . . He said he slipped into my exhibition incognito last year – and it was the best new work he's ever seen! He wants to come and have another look at the paintings tomorrow – he wants to buy some – and he's been working very hard to organize a major exhibition for me at the Tate Modern and they've finally agreed, it's going to be next month!'

'That's fantastic, darling!' my dad said.

'He said all that conceptual stuff – sharks in tanks and all that – everyone's fed up with that now. They want good old-fashioned paintings like mine, executed with skill and technique!'

Maeve's like, 'You sure it's not a trick? Someone imitating Bernard Souter's voice?'

'Who's Bernard Spouter?' Ben asked, scratching his head. He's had nits ever since he started nursery. And that was three years ago. He gets nit-combed every night but they always come back.

Some of the glee faded from Mum's face. 'Oh . . . I suppose it could be a hoax. But who would be cruel enough to do that?'

'People are horrible, Mum,' Maeve said. 'I thought that was a well-known fact.'

'I bet it's not a hoax,' I said.

'What's a hoax?' Ben asked, still scratching.

'You can't trust anyone,' Maeve said. 'No one. No one at all.'

Her phone gave a little twiddly noise. She pulled it out to read the text. Her face went as dazed and pink as Mum's had just done.

'What is it?' Dad asked.

'It's from Stefan!'

'What? Bumgarner?' Dad said. He's never been able to get over Bumgarner's name. Well, none of us have, really.

'What's he say?' Mum asked. 'Looks like good news.'

'Yeah, it's . . . you could say that, yeah,' Maeve said. But she didn't read the text out. She didn't need to, I knew what it said:

Ive been thinking what an idiot ive been. u r the only girl 4 me ever, ive been so miserable since we split, I cant believe what a moron I was. u r the best girl in the world and I am just a stupid idiot. And Josephine is horrible and smelly. Would u take me back? Please? Even though I dont deserve it? Cos I luv u Maeve, I truly do.

'You sure it's not a hoax?' I asked.

But I was only winding her up. It wasn't a hoax. For once, everyone was going to get what they wanted. And it felt good.

The next person to sort out was Ben. Not that he had any real problems. You don't really when you're six, only those nits, but I thought I might as well get rid of them for him. Really destroy them. Eradicate them. Obliterate them once and for all.

After we'd eaten, and Maeve had gone upstairs to phone all her friends and Mum and Dad were in the kitchen stacking the dishwasher, I said, 'I'll give Ben his bath and nit-comb him tonight.'

'Oh, you don't have to do that, Sam,' Mum said.

'Why not?' said Dad. 'Let him do it. We can settle down on the sofa and finish the wine in front of the telly!'

I sat on the toilet seat. Ben was in the bath, telling me a long story about what had happened in school that day. 'Fatima said I shouldn't be on top table for Maths so I asked her what seven and seven was and she said seventy-seven and I said don't be silly that's wrong and she said she was only joking so I said what's the real answer then and she said she knew but she wasn't going to say so I said it's fourteen actually and she said she knew that all along and then she went round telling everyone I didn't know what seven and seven was and I was just telling her off for saying fibs about me and then Miss told me off for talking and that wasn't fair because she told *me* off but not Fatima and said if I kept talking I'd have to be moved off the top Maths table away from all my friends and Fatima's not even my friend!'

'Yeah, that's terrible.' He's always going on about

this Fatima girl. I think they fancy each other a bit, that's why they're always winding each other up.

'If they take me off the top Maths table it's not fair. Then Fatima will laugh at me. She's already on the top Literacy table and I'm not.'

'Listen, Ben, keep still. I'm gonna nitcomb you in a special way today.'

'What you gonna do?'

I hesitated a bit. I hadn't been planning to tell him, but now I thought if I didn't he'd wonder where I'd disappeared to and call out for Mum and Dad. Also he might scratch his head and squash me.

'Listen, Ben, don't be alarmed—'

'Like an alarm clock?'

'Yeah, don't be alarmed like an alarm clock. I'm gonna go tiny and go in your hair and hunt those nits down.'

Now, of course I didn't need to do this. I could have just wished the nits would vanish. But I wanted to make an adventure out of it. A quest. Otherwise, I thought, life would get too boring if you never had to actually *do* anything. OK, the ant-killing hadn't been as much fun as I'd expected. But this was different. Those nits had been driving Ben mad for years. They deserved their comeuppance. And I was going to be the one to give it to them.

Ben looked at me in a kind of solemn way. 'That's impossible.'

'I know it is.'

'If it's impossible you can't do it.'

'Yes I can, because I'm magic.'

'If you're magic, turn into a helicopter.'

'I'll *get* you a helicopter, if you just sit still and don't scratch your head, all right?'

'What colour helicopter?'

'Any colour.'

'Can I have a helicopter that's got spots like a leopard?'

'Yeah, if you just sit still and don't scratch your head, all right?'

Ben nodded. 'All right.'

'In a second I'm gonna go so small you won't see me,' I said. 'But I wish you won't be scared, OK?'

'I won't be scared.'

'No, you won't. Right, so I wish I was really small, about twice as big as a nit, and I wish I was in Ben's hair, and I wish I had a sharp, shining sword of just the right size!'

The next instant I was in a brown forest, with big strands of hair as thick as my arm sprouting up all around me, droplets of water as big as coconuts clinging to them and a forest floor of pink scalp.

I heard Ben's voice, loud and echoey in the tiled bathroom, commentating on the situation quite calmly. 'Sam's gone. He's gone small. He's in my hair. He's killing nits.'

I made my way through the forest, following the pink paths through the giant hairs, looking all around, sword at the ready. I heard a kind of scritching noise and steered towards it. A moment later I came face to face with my first nit. Or head louse, to use the correct terminology. The nits are the egg cases, I know that really. But everyone just says nits for the whole lot, don't they?

Well, I'd thought ants were ugly. But compared to nits, the ants were film stars. Beauty queens. Visions of loveliness.

The nit, or louse, in front of me, was around the size of a large dog. It had two wiggling antennae, six waving legs that ended in claws, and a fat tail like a fish. It looked like it was made out of some sort of semi-transparent jelly. You could see all the blood swirling around inside it. Its face – well, I don't know whether to call it a face, exactly – was soft and doughy, with a black oval eye on each side. Like something out of a nightmare. Its mouth parts were plugged into Sam's scalp and it was sucking greedily. You couldn't imagine a more repulsive creature. No one could like it. Even their own mothers don't like them. They just lay their eggs and crawl off to a different part of the head.

I walked right up to it. The stupid, dumb creature just carried on sucking.

'This is the end of the line for you, nit!' I said.

But I don't think it heard because they don't have any ears. I plunged my shining sword into its side. A pale liquid gushed out, streaked with blood. The creature wriggled, but carried on sucking. I cut its head off, and it finally stopped.

When I'd first thought of this scenario, I'd imagined that every time I killed one I'd throw it off Sam's head to land in the bathwater. But that wasn't possible. It was too big and I was too small and I'd never get it past the forest of hairs. I'd just have to let the corpses lie where they fell and comb them out after.

One down. Lots more to go.

I stalked through the forest, slaying the monsters as I found them. None of them put up any resistance. They were too dumb to know what was going on. They were just bloodsuckers, that was all they could do. I came upon their white, football-sized eggs, singly or in clusters, stuck on to the side of hairs, and punctured every one I saw.

The longer it went on, though, the less I liked it. I'd thought this would be an adventure, but there was no excitement in it. And I kept having this unpleasant thought that in a way I was lowering myself to the level of the nits. They went around sucking blood and I went around stabbing them, and was there really much difference?

I'd killed about ten, I s'pose, when I decided to call it a day. This could go on for a long time – Mum had announced she'd combed out eighty-five only the other night – and it was pointless. All I had to do was wish the nits were gone, after all. There was no need to personally hand-slaughter them.

So, I wished Ben's head was clear of all lice and I wished that I was back to normal size and sitting on the toilet seat again.

'All gone?' Ben asked, when I reappeared.

'All gone.'

'Where's my leopard helicopter, then?'

'Coming up.'

So that was it, everyone in my family had got what they wanted. Except me.

But what did I want?

Later that night, I was lying in bed reading some Marvel comics I'd wished for. After a while I got tired of reading and wished the superheroes and supervillains would come to life – but in miniature, the same size as they were in the comics – and act out their battles for me at the foot of my bed. It was great fun watching the Fantastic Four slugging it out with Doctor Doom on my duvet.

I'd always wanted to be a superhero.

Yeah. *That* was what I wanted.

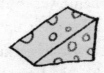

CHAPTER EIGHT

I t was a pretty cool costume. I had a blue mask over my eyes, and a blue leotard, with blue boots, yellow tights and a yellow cape. Oh, yeah, and the blue leotard had yellow stars on it. I looked at myself in the mirror – I'd never had a full-length mirror in my room, but it was simple enough to wish for one – and thought, *Yeah, looks good.* The only things missing were the bulging muscles that superheroes tend to have, so I wished for a complete set: pecs, biceps, triceps, an awesome six-pack, the works. I looked at myself in the mirror again, and was impressed. You wouldn't want to tangle with me.

Now I had to think of what super-powers to have. Ability to fly, obviously, that was a no-brainer. And super-strength, another gimme. What else, what else? The ability to go through walls like a ghost, that was a good one. And the power to run super fast, faster than a cheetah. And keep it up indefinitely. Better than a cheetah, because they get tired after about four hundred metres. I also wished for stretchy arms and legs like Mr Fantastic. And the ability to survive indefinitely without breathing, and to withstand extremes of heat and cold, and to be immune to pain, and have a body that automatically went diamond-hard if anyone hit me or kicked me or smote me a blow of any kind. And I'd better be bullet-proof and bomb-proof and fire-proof too, 'cause as a superhero I was bound to make a few enemies. That made me pretty much invincible. Finally, just for fun, I wished to be able to burrow underground like a mole.

Now I just had to think of a name.

Sam-Man?

Er, no.

Er . . .

Awesome Man?

Awesome Man!

Now to start crime-busting!

It was the morning after I'd got rid of Ben's nits and saved Dad's job, etc. Obviously I'd need the day off school to start my career as a superhero, so I wished the school was closed for the day because the boiler had broken down. I looked out of the window. It was a grey, drizzly day which didn't look like it would be a whole lot of fun to fly through. So I wished it was nice and sunny, twenty degrees with a light breeze.

I tugged at the window to open it, but it was a bit stiff. So I made a wish and it swung open obediently. I realized then that I'd never need to open a window manually again. Or a door. I could just wish they were already open. Actually I didn't even need to do that. I didn't need windows or doors *at all*. I could just wish to be outside (or inside) whenever I wanted . . .

Anyway, I launched myself through the open window and flew out into the fresh morning air.

I stretched out my arms in front of me like Superman. I felt the wind rushing past my ears and my cape fluttering out behind me. The streets and trees and houses glided past below. I felt weightless and completely free. It was like those flying dreams I used to have when I was a little kid.

I scanned the streets below for crime. Not much going on down there, though. Shops opening their shutters. People on their way to work, driving cars, hopping on and off buses. A few looked up and noticed me, and then more and more, and soon there were crowds of people gawping and pointing up at me. I waved at them.

Well, I flew around for a bit, waiting for something to kick off so I could fly down and stop it. Nothing happened. Well, nothing illegal. Listening to the news sometimes you'd think we lived in some sort of a war zone, with people being attacked and killed all over the place. It's not till you fly around above a whole town and watch it in action that you realize how law-abiding people are most of the time. They just go round getting on with their lives. No one even jumped a red light.

The morning dragged on. I got tired of waiting. I was sure there *must* be some crimes going on somewhere.

'I wish I was wherever the nearest person breaking

the law is,' I said aloud.

Whoosh! I landed on the pavement near a bloke parking his car on double-yellow lines.

Hmm . . . It wasn't really the type of crime I'd been imagining. I mean, I don't think Batman gets called on the hotline whenever someone double-parks in Gotham City. I'd have preferred a bank job, to be honest. For a moment I thought of wishing for one, but then I realized that would be pretty silly. A super-hero who only solves crimes he's wished for himself. Like, Pointless Man.

Oh well. You have to work with what you get.

'Hold it,' I said, as the bloke got out of his car. He was a black bloke with glasses and a suit and tie. 'You can't park there.'

'It's only for a minute, I need to get something in that shop—'

'Sorry, that's not allowed.'

'Look, why don't you mind your own business?'

'It is my business, my friend, my duty is to uphold the law—'

'Are you a traffic warden?'

'You'll have to move that car.'

'They've changed the uniform if you are!'

'Never mind about that—'

'That's the most ridiculous uniform I've ever seen. And we're paying for that out of our council tax? It's a disgrace!'

'Look, I'm not a traffic warden—'

'What uniform is it, then?'

'It's not a uniform, it's a costume.'

'A fancy dress costume?'

'No, it's *my* costume. The costume of . . . *Awesome Man*!'

The bloke started to look up and down the street. 'This is one of those TV programmes, isn't it? Where they play tricks on unsuspecting members of the public? Where are the cameras?'

'There aren't any cameras!'

'I bet they're in that van, aren't they?' He started smiling and waving at a van on the other side of the road. 'Hello Mum!'

I was getting a bit fed up. I didn't come into the superhero game for this sort of thing. Iron Man doesn't spend his time arguing with people on pavements, trying to get them to take him seriously, does he? It was . . . undignified. And it wasn't like I really gave a monkey's where the guy parked his car anyway.

'All right,' I said. 'I've had enough of this. You can park your car where you like, but if you get a ticket, don't blame me.'

And then I launched myself up from the pavement and zoomed into the sky. I glanced down when I was above roof height and the bloke was goggling up at me in disbelief.

I flew on. I should explain about how it felt to fly. It didn't take any effort at all – it wasn't like swimming. I just pointed in the direction I wanted to fly and that's the direction I went in. And I could go faster or slower just by thinking about it. It was like if you decide to raise your hand, and it goes up – you don't really know how, it just does.

Then, at last, I looked down and saw something going on in an alley. Two figures, one big and one small, and the big one had pushed the little one up against a wall.

'This looks like a job for Awesome Man!' I said to myself.

I dived down and landed beside them with a thump.

The bigger one looked round with a start, and I recognized him.

'Hiya Scorpus. Just thought I'd drop by.'

He had one hand round the smaller boy's neck, and the other hand clenched in a fist, cocked and ready to go. The smaller boy was a blond kid with spots. Really bad spots. Quite inflamed. And I thought, *That's pretty bad luck, not only do you get a seriously bad skin day but then you get mugged into the bargain.*

Scorpus was like, 'Who are you? How do you know my name?'

'I'm Awesome Man. Awesome Man knows all kinds of stuff!'

'Yeah? Well, get lost and mind your own business, and you won't get hurt!'

'*I* won't get hurt. It's you I'm worried about.'

I grabbed hold of his arm and squeezed with my super-strength. Scorpus's pale face went even paler. He let go of the kid.

'Are you OK?' I said to the boy. 'What was he doing to you?'

'Tryin'a steal my phone. And my money.'

I turned to stare at Scorpus. I was still holding his arm, and I squeezed it a bit tighter. Scorpus sucked in his breath and swore. He twisted and kneed me extremely hard in the privates. There was a painful-sounding *thunk*. Not painful to me, of course, because thanks to my super-powers my body had gone diamond-hard at the crucial moment.

Scorpus was like, 'Aaaaghh!' He reeled off a string of swear words. 'My knee. I think it's broke!'

'It's not broken at all, Scorpus! It's just severely bruised. And serves you right anyway.' I turned back to the kid. 'Are you OK?'

The kid nodded.

'Good. You can go then. Oh, just one thing – I wish all your spots were gone.'

All the angry, red spots on his cheeks and chin vanished, leaving his skin all smooth and fresh, like a baby's bum. He put his hand up to his face and looked amazed. 'Awesome!'

'All part of the service. That's why they call me . . . Awesome Man!'

The fresh-faced kid ran off down the alley.

'Now, what am I gonna do with you, Scorpus? You gotta stop mugging people. Mugging is . . . well, it's a mug's game!'

'Let . . . go . . . my arm.' He spoke in little gasps, through gritted teeth.

I let go. His good arm rubbed the bad arm, while the bad arm massaged his knee.

'Why do you do it, Scorpus?'

He swore at me again. 'Mind your own business, or I'll . . .'

'You'll never get anywhere being a mugger,' I told him. 'No one likes muggers. They never get rich. They never get OBEs or knighthoods. They don't get streets or buildings named after them. We don't put their pictures on ten-pound notes or anything.'

'Who are you? I know that voice.'

'It's me.' I pushed my mask back on to my head. 'Sam Polkinghorne. I already battered you once, at school, remember?'

He narrowed his eyes and swore at me again.

'Swearing's the sign of a small vocabulary, Scorpus.' (That's what my dad says, anyway. I don't know if it's true but I thought it sounded good.) 'Now let me ask you again. Why go round mugging people?'

'Let me put it like this,' Scorpus began, and then he suddenly jabbed me in the throat, with straight, stiff fingers. My diamond-hard powers kicked in automatically and he broke his fingernails. 'Ow!' he howled. 'Oooooowwwww!'

I started to lose patience. I gripped Scorpus round the middle and rose up into the air, till we were level with the tops of the lamp posts.

'Answer my question, Scorpus, or I'll drop you!'

'Help!' shouted Scorpus.

'You can help yourself, if you just answer me. Why do you do it?'

I felt Scorpus go limp. He stopped struggling, and gave a great big sigh, as if he'd just given up on everything.

'I – I have to,' he said.

'What do you mean? 'Course you don't have to.'

'I do. I need the money.'

'What for?'

'Everything! Food. Clothes. Trainers. My phone.'

'Your parents are s'posed to buy those things . . .'

Scorpus gave a bitter laugh. 'Yeah, right. My dad gives me nothing – *nothing*. Not even dinner money. He says I have to learn to fend for myself. Like he did.'

'He wouldn't like it if he knew you were out robbing people.'

'What you going on about? *'Course* he'd like it.'

Actually, from what I'd heard about Scorpus's dad that was probably true. 'But – what about your mum?'

Scorpus laughed that bitter laugh again. 'If you think my mum would dare to disagree with my dad about anything – well, you don't know him, that's all.'

'Well, what are we gonna do, then? You can't carry on mugging people.'

'I dunno. I got to eat, don't I?'

This was all getting a bit more complicated than I'd expected. In the comics, superheroes just beat the villains up. They don't have to start solving their family problems. They simply don't get involved in that side of things.

'Will you put me down now?' said Scorpus.

I drifted to the ground again and let him go. 'Listen,' I said. 'I'll give you some cash to tide you over.' I wished for fifty quid and gave it to him. 'S'pose I go and see your dad – tell him to start being nice to you, feed you properly, give you an allowance. Would that be OK?'

Scorpus laughed. 'Good luck with that!'

'Luck doesn't come into it,' I said. 'You're talking to Awesome Man!'

Scorpus's home was a two-bedroom flat in a run-down estate on the edge of town. There was litter all over the ground, graffiti on the walls, and scaly, diseased pigeons pecking about among the rubbish. As I flew down, I wished it was all tidied up, with the litter in bins, the graffiti cleaned away and the pigeons moved on. I also wished for some nice flower beds full of tulips, and for all the front doors to be newly painted in bright colours, so I'd done a pretty good job even before I got to knocking on Scorpus's door.

After I knocked there was a long pause. I hate waiting for things, always have, so I wished he'd come and open the door straight away. (I'd never have to wait for anything again, I realized. No more hanging around at bus stops for buses that never came. Although come to think of it, I'd never need to catch a bus again, either.)

The door was flung open and there stood Old Man – I realized I didn't know what his surname was, and quickly wished that I did. *Bartrum,* the newsreader's voice in my head said. So, there stood Old Man Bartrum.

'Mr Bartrum?'

He was a big man, tall and gangly with a sharp face like a hatchet. His head was shaved and his arms were covered in tats. His biceps were unexpectedly big and meaty and I guessed he probably worked out. But he also had a bit of a paunch so I guessed he probably called in at the chip shop on the way home from the gym. He had a gold tooth in the front of his mouth.

'Who wants to know?'

'Me. Well, I don't wanna know 'cause I already know actually. I've come to have a word with you.'

'Who are you? And why are you dressed up like – what *are* you dressed up like? Some sort of cheer-leader?'

'I'm Awesome Man and this is my costume—'

'Step off.' And he slammed the door on me.

I immediately wished it would bounce back open, of course.

He stood there glaring at me. 'I said, step *off*!'

Once again he slammed the door and again I wished for it to bounce straight back open.

'We can keep this up all day if you want,' I said. 'But why don't you just listen to what I have to say? It'll be quicker.'

'I'll tell you what'll be quicker,' Bartrum growled. You often read in books about people growling when they get angry. I'd never really heard it before. He deliberately deepened his voice and put a sort of gritty edge into it, if you know what I mean. 'It'll be quicker if you just clear off before you leave in an ambulance.'

'I need to speak to you about your son—'

'You leave my boy out of this! He ain't done nothing, d'you hear me? And if he did it ain't my fault. And I don't even have a son, anyway. If you've come here to complain about him, I'll give you something to complain about! You come round here, knocking on my door – the nerve of it! The liberty!'

I could see he was working himself into a fury. 'Look,' I said, 'calm down—'

'Calm down? You're asking for a clock on the snot-box, you are!'

'No I'm not—'

And the next moment, he clocked me on the snotbox. The nose, I mean. Which of course turned diamond-hard at the moment of impact.

Blood spurted from his knuckles. He staggered back, clutching his hand and cursing.

'I'll tell you what, Mr Bartrum, why don't I come in and we can discuss this in a more civilized manner?'

'We could do that, yeah, or we could try . . . *this*!'

He hit me as hard as he could in the stomach with his other hand, and then doubled up in agony, each injured hand tucked beneath the opposite arm.

'Aaaargh!'

'Look, I'm sorry about this, but if you'd stop hitting me, you wouldn't keep hurting yourself. Tell you what, I wish we were sitting down in your living room.'

The room was a bit of a tip. Empty beer cans and pizza boxes all over the place. I was sitting on an armchair on top of a plate with crumbs on it, which I had to move out from under me. Old Man Bartrum was on the sofa opposite, staring at me with a combination of fear, hatred and bewilderment.

'How did you do that?'

'I'm Awesome Man. It's all in a day's work for me. Listen, I want to talk to you about Scorpus. From what I hear, you treat him very badly. You don't give him any dinner money and he has to buy his own clothes.'

'That's none of your business. And it's all lies.'

'Is it, Mr Bartrum? Is it?'

'Why don't you go away before I smash your face in?'

'Look, can't we just discuss this sensibly? What's the matter with you?'

'I've got anger management issues,' Bartrum said. 'That's what the prison psychologist told me.'

'Did they? And what did *you* say?'

'I didn't say nothing. I clocked him on the snotbox.'

I sighed. How was I ever going to get through to him? 'Look, you've got to start being nicer to your son, and your wife, OK?'

'I haven't got a wife.'

'Well, your girlfriend or whatever. You gotta be nice to them.'

'I'm always nice to them.' He looked at me with big sincere eyes. 'I'm a good person, I am. Deep down.'

'Is that right?'

'I tell you what,' Bartrum said, suddenly completely changing his manner and smiling at me, his gold tooth glinting. 'Do you want a cup of tea and a biscuit? I got some Hobnobs.'

I didn't really want tea and biscuits, but it was the first sign of reasonable behaviour he'd displayed so I thought I'd better go along with it. 'All right then. Thanks.'

He went out into the kitchen.

I called after him. 'I just came to say, you've got to start treating your son better. Look after him, you know? Also, your girlfriend. I hear she's scared of you. That's not a healthy relationship, Mr Bartrum.'

All I could hear from the kitchen was the sound of rummaging around in cupboards.

'Are you listening to me, Mr Bartrum?'

'Oh yes, I'm listening. It's very interesting, what you're saying.'

Then he ran out of the kitchen with a frying pan in his hand and smashed me over the head with it.

The handle of the frying pan broke. Bartrum howled in pain and collapsed on to the sofa. The vibration of the impact must have hurt his already-damaged hand. And even I gave a sort of grunt of discomfort. Of course the frying pan hadn't actually hurt my diamond-hard head, but it made a very loud clanging noise, and the blow reverberated in my skull and made me feel dizzy.

What could you do with a person like this? He was an out-and-out psycho. There was no way I could persuade him to mend his ways, unless . . .

Of course. Unless.

'I wish you'd be nice to your son and partner, OK?'

'OK,' said Bartrum mildly.

'I wish you'd give them money when they need it, OK?'

'OK.'

There was a bit of a silence. Mission accomplished, I realized.

'Well, I'll be off then.'

'Sure you won't stay for tea?'

'Nah, got a few things to do.'

And I wished myself back in my bedroom.

Then I realized that my digestive system was actually feeling a bit cheated, so I wished for a nice cup of tea and a plate of Hobnobs.

CHAPTER NINE

As I drank the tea and ate the Hobnobs while sitting on my bed, I pondered on being a superhero. There was something pointless about it when you had a million wishes at your disposal. Or almost a million, whatever it was. I'd solved the Bartrum problem just by wishing he'd be nice. I didn't need to go and confront the man. I could have done it sitting in my bedroom. I didn't need the costume, didn't need to be able to fly. Nor did I need the cheetah-like running speed or the stretchy arms and legs. I didn't need any of it.

I wished I didn't have the costume any more. It

was a silly costume anyway. And I wished away the super-powers too. Because *they* were pointless as well. Flying had been fun for a while, but I didn't need it. Why fly anywhere? I could just wish I was already there. It was a pity, maybe, that I'd never got to use my burrowing powers. But again, what was the point of them? If I ever needed to get anything that was buried underground I could just wish it was above ground, not go squirming down after it like a giant mole.

My phone went off.

'Hi Evan.'

'Was that you who closed the school down today?'

'Yeah, I did that.'

'Cool. What you doing today then?'

'Dunno. Wanna come over?'

'Yeah, sure.'

'Hold tight then. I wish Evan was here.'

He materialized in the middle of the bedroom, and his eyes immediately landed on the plate of chocolate Hobnobs. 'Oh, good, can I have one?'

'Yeah, get stuck in.'

There were three biscuits left and he polished them off in about forty-five seconds. I wondered whether to wish for a few more for him, but decided not to.

'Sam?'

'Yeah?'

'What I was saying yesterday – about guessing what I want you to wish for . . .'

To be honest, what with one thing and another, this had completely slipped my mind.

'I just wanted you to figure it out for yourself,' Evan said. 'I felt kind of awkward and – I sort of thought the wish might work better if it came from you. I dunno. But now – I have to ask you straight out . . .'

And then the whole scenario flashed into my mind. 'Your dad!' I said.

Evan nodded. 'My dad.' His voice sort of quivered. 'He's really ill, Sam.' I looked, and saw his eyes were full of silver tears. 'He's dying.'

'Oh, I . . . oh my God. Oh, Evan,' I said.

I felt a horrible stab of guilt. Why hadn't I thought of this before? I knew how ill Evan's dad was. The last time I'd seen him was a few weeks ago, just after he came out of hospital, and he looked really thin and grey and weak. The only thing I can say in my defence is that Evan didn't talk about it much, and when he mentioned his dad he tended to speak about things his dad said or did or liked, not about the illness. And in day-to-day life Evan seemed normal, having a laugh and a joke and playing games like everyone else. But maybe that's how people deal with it. The thought of Evan pretending to feel normal when all the time his heart was breaking inside made me feel even worse.

'Evan, I'm sorry,' I said. 'I should have realized. Of course I'll wish he's better!'

His face lit up, like the sun breaking through rain clouds. If faces were skies, his would have had a rainbow all over it.

'Serious?'

'Yeah. Serious. I wish Evan's dad was completely better, right now!'

'And that's it?' Evan said.

'That's it!'

'He's better already?'

'That's what I wished for. And my wishes come true!'

'What's he doing?'

'Let's find out . . . I wish I knew what Evan's dad is

up to.'

The newsreader's voice intoned inside my head, *He's just thrown back the bedclothes, got up and announced he's going to mow the lawn.*

I passed this on to Evan.

'That grass has got really long,' Evan said. 'I better go and give him a hand!'

'Do you want a few biscuits to take?'

'Biscuits? I don't need biscuits *now*, do I?' And then I realized that it was only in the last couple of years, while his dad was ill, that Evan had got over-weight. He must have been comfort-eating all that time.

'Wait a minute, though,' Evan said. 'I'll take some for my dad, I bet he'll have his appetite back!'

I wished for a speciality box of biscuits with chocolate and icing on, and thrust it into Evan's arms.

'Want me to wish you were there?' I asked.

'No, I . . . think I'll walk.'

'Sure.'

I watched him through the window as he left with the box of biscuits under his arm. He didn't walk, though. He ran.

CHAPTER TEN

I'd done a good thing for Evan, even though I'd taken my time about it, and I felt kind of pleased with myself. I imagined him going home, seeing his dad, flying into his arms. I waited for a while, thinking Evan would text or phone about it, but he didn't, so I s'pose he was too busy getting used to having his dad back in full health again, and I couldn't blame him.

I sat in my room and wondered what to do next. No one else was around. Ben and Maeve were at school and college, dad was at work, and mum was in the shed getting her paintings ready for Bernard

Souter. He was coming round tonight.

It was getting on for lunchtime, and I was feeling a bit peckish. There's this dish Mum sometimes makes, Chicken Supreme, which is pieces of chicken breast in a white, creamy sauce with rice, and I really like it. I don't know what made me think of it just then, but I wished for a big plate of it. I was about to eat it on a tray on my knees sitting on my bed, and then I thought, *Come on, you can do better than that*, so I wished I was sitting up in the director's box at White Hart Lane, watching Tottenham Hotspur play Arsenal. I had the box all to myself, and I wished Spurs would win seven-nil, and I scoffed the Chicken Supreme listening to the roar of the crowd as the goals flew in. Which was kind of fun. But not as much fun as it would have been if I hadn't wished for it. Of course if I hadn't wished for it, it wouldn't have happened. The trouble was it wasn't a surprise. Once I'd made the wish, it was, you know, inevitable, just like Wednesday following Tuesday.

And I realized that surprises were a thing of the past for me, now that I had my wishes. No surprises, no suspense, no uncertainty. No feeling of joy at an unexpected piece of good luck. No sense of relief when something that looked like it was going to turn out badly turned out OK. Reality wasn't something I could bump into any more. It was something that did what I told it.

Was that even a proper life at all?

The referee blew his whistle for full time. I wished that Tottenham would win the Premier League that season. At least that would surprise quite a few people, even if I wasn't one of them.

I wished myself back in my bedroom. I was actually starting to feel a bit bored, which is ridiculous when you've got almost a million wishes at your disposal. What could I do?

The superhero thing. Maybe I hadn't explored that properly yet. Obviously Scorpus and Old Man Bartrum weren't worthy opponents. They were pushovers. I needed someone who was more of a match for me.

Most superheroes have some kind of arch-enemy. Like, Batman has the Joker and Spiderman has the Green Goblin and the Fantastic Four have Doctor Doom. And the arch-enemy has the power to hurt them, threaten them, frustrate them. The superhero always wins in the end, but the arch-enemy can give them a pretty hard time along the way. And even when the superhero finally triumphs, the arch-enemy usually slips away with a promise to come back and make trouble another day. That's part of the fun of it.

I needed an enemy who could make a fight of it.

First, I wished for all my powers back, the same ones as before, but I gave myself a different costume. I wished I was dressed all in black leather, with lots of silver studs and stars and stuff, and a big silver letter A on my chest. I thought it looked a bit tougher, somehow. More manly.

Now I needed an arch-enemy.

This was going to be fun. You know, I've often thought when I leave school I'd like to get a job writing stories for comics. Come to think of it, I could just wish that was my job, if I was serious. But I dunno. I didn't *need* a job now, did I?

I forced my thoughts back to my arch-enemy. I wished first of all that he could fly and was super strong. But he needed something different, something to make him unique . . . I thought back to Bartrum hitting me with a frying pan. How about if my arch-enemy had frying pans for hands? No, something a bit deadlier, maybe. Hammers! With which he battered his opponents. Super-strong hammers that didn't break. Hammer Man? Hammerhand? No, wait, *one* hand could be a hammer. The other one could be a circular saw. And suddenly I got the whole concept: Power-Tool Man! His head was a pneumatic drill. His body was a workbench. His legs were those things that workmen use to flatten tarmac, what are they called? Piledrivers, that's it.

'I wish Power-Tool Man existed, and I wish he was coming to get me!'

There was a splintering crash as my bedroom door flew off its hinges.

There stood Power-Tool Man. His power-drill head was pointing straight at me, twirling round and round. His circular-saw arm was raised.

'Hello Mr so-called Awesome Man!' he said in a horrible, whiny drill voice. 'Let us see how awesome you are ven you are all smeshed into liddle tiny bits.' He had a German accent, I don't know why.

'Bring it on, Power-Tool Man. If you think you're hard enough.'

'Oh, *ja*, I sink I vill be hard enoff to deal vid you. My power-tools are all diamond-tipped, you know.'

Diamond-tipped! The only thing hard enough to

cut another diamond!

He lunged at me with unexpected speed. I dodged and his whirring drill bit missed me by millimetres. As he went past I clouted him with all my force on the side of his head. He fell on to my bed and his circular saw ripped the mattress in two. Before he could regain his feet I leapt on him, grabbed him by the arms and flew out of the window with him.

As we zoomed up into the clear blue sky he smashed me repeatedly on the side of the head with his hammer-hand. The diamond-tipped hammer was making dents in me, I could feel it. That couldn't be good.

'You like dis, *ja*?'

'Not much – but tell me how you like . . . *this*!'

We were about a hundred metres up in the air, and I let go of him. I expected him to fall and hit the ground with a sickening clang, but somehow I'd forgotten that he could fly, just like me, so instead of falling he just looped the loop, came up behind me and gave me a massive kick with one of his piledriver legs. I flew across the sky, out of control, arms waving helplessly.

'*Ja*, I am liking dis, it is *sehr gut*!'

'I wish you'd stop talking in that stupid accent!'

'What stupid accent?' he said, in a perfectly normal English accent.

'I'm not here to give you elocution lessons, Power-Tool Man. I'm here to knock you into a pile of scrap metal!'

I steadied myself, thrust my fists out in front of me and power-dived at him at top speed. He didn't try to get out of the way but flew straight towards me.

We met with a terrific clatter in the middle of the sky and bounced apart. But he recovered first. I was still spinning in the air when I felt his drill bite into my chest. At the same time the circular saw started to chew into my neck, and the hammer-hand was whacking me on the back of the head.

This was . . . too much. 'I wish you couldn't fly any more, Power-Tool Man,' I shouted, and immediately he plunged away from me and spiralled towards the earth. He hit the ground with a crash that was loud even from a hundred metres up.

He wasn't hurt though, what with being super strong. He bounced straight back up on to his feet. I zoomed down towards him. He started winding his hammer-hand up, whirling it round to get ready for a mighty blow. But I wasn't having it. 'I wish you were as weak as a kitten!' I said. So he stood there, all helpless and tottering, not strong enough even to raise his power-tool arms. I landed beside him and gave him a little push in his workbench-chest and he fell on his back.

'Do you surrender, Power-Tool Man?'

'No, I'll never surrender!'

'I wish you would.'

'Oh, all right, I surrender, then.'

'Another awesome victory for Awesome Man!' I said. But it didn't feel all that awesome. I was fed up. 'I wish you didn't exist any more, Power-Tool Man.'

'I don't.'

And he was gone.

I wished my bedroom was all back to normal again. Then I went downstairs to watch telly for a bit, and amused myself by making the actors and presenters say stupid things and insult each other. So that was quite funny. It passed the time, anyway.

Things looked up a bit later when my family started coming home. Mum went to get Ben from school at three. He was in a super-good mood, full of his day.

'Guess what happened at school, Sam?' he shouted as soon as he got into the hall. Obviously I knew what had happened 'cause I'd wished for it, but I said, 'What?'

'I got put on top table for Literacy!'

'Did you?'

'He did,' Mum said. 'Miss Martinez said she'd never seen anything like it. She said he was reading aloud from *Great Expectations*!'

'Where'd you get that from, then?'

'Dunno, I just found it in my book bag. I dunno where it came from. But I can read it! I can read anything! I just look at the words and they all make sense, it's like magic!'

'Cool.'

'They did a test,' my mum said. 'Miss Martinez says he's got a reading age of fourteen!'

'Yeah, and Fatima was really fed up!' Ben added. He started dancing around the hall chanting, 'In your face, Fatima!' until Mum gave him a prod to make him shut up.

Ben went upstairs to play with his new remote-controlled helicopter. What he didn't know was I'd wished for a miniature leopard to pilot it, and the leopard could talk and say things like 'Altitude six hundred metres' and 'Just bringing her into land', and wave its paw at him as it flew by. I listened outside his room and heard his squeaks of excitement.

'Sam!' he said. 'Come and see this!'

I went in and saw the little leopard flying about. 'Excellent weather conditions for flying today!' it squeaked. 'Hello Ben!'

'This is the best helicopter ever!' Ben said.

'Yeah, but don't tell Mum and Dad about it. It's our secret.'

'Why? 'Cause it's magic?'

'Yes, Ben. 'Cause it's magic.'

When Maeve got in from sixth-form college she was in a super-good mood too.

She ruffled my hair as she came into the living room. 'All right, Sam?'

'Yeah, fine.'

'How was school?'

'We got the day off today. Boiler broke down.'

'That was a result, wasn't it? Still, it's not too bad there, is it?'

'It's OK.'

'Listen, I'm sorry if I talked it up a bit, you know. I was only teasing.'

'No worries. How was your day?'

'Fantastic!'

'Why?'

I knew why, obviously, because I'd made a few wishes, but I wanted to hear how they'd worked out.

It was all going swimmingly with Stefan Bumgarner. He was totally crazy about her and went around holding her hand all day, which he never used to like doing, but now it was as if he wanted to advertise his love to the whole world. Also, he'd bought them both tickets to see some weird French circus where they ride motorbikes on tightropes and juggle chainsaws to the accompaniment of loud rock music and crazy laser displays, which she'd always wanted to go and see.

'Sounds great.'

'Yep. Life's sweet!' She smiled, and I realized how pretty she was when her face wasn't all creased up in a scowl.

Mum was in the kitchen now, cooking supper, and singing at the top of her voice. She couldn't wait for

Bernard Souter to turn up.

A key turned in the front door and my dad came in. I went into the hall to greet him.

'Hey Sam!' He gave me a hug. 'You'll never believe what happened to me today!'

'What?'

'I have to tell your mum this!' I followed him into the kitchen. 'Roger Haggerston came to my office today, and he said I was so good at my job that he wanted to promote me – to *his* job! He's going to step down, because he says he knows I'm the better man!'

'Did he really say that?'

'His exact words. "You're the better man by far", he said.'

'Amazing!'

'My salary's going to double, and I'm going to have a much bigger office, with a drinks cabinet and a view of the river.'

'Fantastic!'

The doorbell rang. Mum ran to open it, and it was Bernard Souter. He was wearing white trousers and a cream-coloured jacket and a sort of candy-striped shirt.

'Good evening, Mr Souter!'

'Oh, please, you must call me Bernard. And I shall call you Susan!'

'Well, you could, but my name's actually Nicola.'

'I beg your pardon, Nicola. Yes, Nicola Polkinghorne is a name that the world will soon know very well indeed! Your wonderful work is like a breath of fresh air in a stale and dusty mausoleum!'

'Yes, that's the effect I've been striving for,' said Mum.

'And where are the pictures? Let us delay no further, I am athirst, I am agog!' He had just about the poshest voice I'd ever heard.

Mum led him through the kitchen and down the garden to the shed at the end. We all trooped after them, to hear what he was going to say. Well, in my case, I knew, but I still trooped along to actually hear him say it.

He walked along the line of paintings, giving little groans and gasps of pleasure and appreciation. He stopped in front of a still life of a loaf of bread on a breadboard with a dish of butter next to it and some crumbs. 'Remarkable!' he murmured. He moved on to a picture of a blackbird on a lawn casting a long shadow that made it look like it was on stilts. 'Wonderful!' Next, he feasted his eyes on a portrait of Ben, which did look like him, but also like a kind of evil goblin. 'Stupendous!'

I should say here that I really don't know much about art, and to be honest I don't know how good my mum's stuff is. But the paintings were all done in nice bright colours and looked more or less like what they were supposed to look like. They looked OK to me. I don't know about 'stupendous', but I've seen worse stuff in galleries, you know?

'Contemporary British art is moribund,' Bernard announced. 'Twitching in its death throes! These wonderful paintings will sweep all that arid, self-indulgent, conceptual nonsense aside. It will be a new dawn for British art – a revolution!'

'Oh, well, you know, that's very nice of you,' Mum said, all grinning and blushing.

'So you think there's enough here for an exhibition?' my dad said.

'Oh, certainly, certainly. *Certainement!* I have arranged for a major exhibition at Tate Modern – and I can assure you it will make everything else there look suddenly very old-fashioned indeed! Now, I am sure that all these pictures will sell, and will fetch very high prices indeed. I am not a rich man – but could I perhaps be permitted the liberty of putting in a bid for one of these wonderful paintings before the exhibition? Otherwise, I fear I shall be swept aside in the rush!'

'Take your pick!' said my mum.

'An impossible decision ... For the first time in my life I truly understand the full force of the expression "spoilt for choice" . . . But on the whole, all things considered, I think . . . this one!' He pointed to the one of the bird with the long-legged shadow. 'How much, dear lady?'

Mum and Dad looked at each other. 'What do you think?' said my dad.

'Er, fifty pounds?' suggested my mum.

'Nonsense!' said Bernard. 'A trifling, piffling sum!'

'Well, I don't know then,' my mum said. 'What about a hundred?'

'Surely you jest? The painting is worth many times that!'

'Five hundred?' my dad said.

'Nowhere near enough!'

'All right then,' said my mum. 'A thousand!'

'You are determined to rob yourself!'

'Five thousand?'

'Make it ten thousand, and we have a deal!' He took out his chequebook and a silver fountain pen, and made out a cheque to Nicola Polkinghorne on the spot. Then he placed a little sticky red dot on the frame of the picture. 'That is to signify the painting has been sold, and after the exhibition it will come to me!'

'That's fantastic, Mum!' Maeve said.

'He should have picked the one of me,' Ben said.

'You're right!' Souter said suddenly. 'That is indeed a wonderful painting and I would be an abject fool not to purchase it while I have the opportunity!' Out came the chequebook and fountain pen again. 'Shall we say ten thousand for this one too?'

CHAPTER ELEVEN

I lay in bed the next morning trying to decide whether to go to school or not. Obviously I could have had the day off, or as many days as I wanted. In fact, I never needed to go to school again if I didn't feel like it. But I decided in the end to go, just for something to do. I didn't bother with all that getting up stuff though, that was a waste of time. I just wished I was already up and dressed and washed and all that. I never needed to do any of that stuff again. That was one of the weird things about having all these wishes – I kept discovering new things I'd never need to do again.

And the thought crossed my mind: *was there* anything *I needed to do now?*

As I went downstairs I could hear Mum singing, 'Oh, what a beautiful morning, oh, what a beautiful day!' When I went into the kitchen she was all smiles, and so were Ben and Maeve. (Dad had already left – couldn't wait to get to his enormous new office with the river view.) It really did make an amazing difference to get up in the morning and see everyone in a good mood, because to be honest at that time of day everyone in our house normally looks about as happy as a bloodhound with a stomach ache.

'What do you want for breakfast, Sam?'

'I wish for a full English.'

'Oh, don't be silly, there's no time for that—'

''Course there is, look it's already done!' I pointed at the heaped plate – bacon, eggs, sausages, black pudding, beans, mushrooms, grilled tomatoes, fried bread – that had appeared on the breakfast table.

'What? How did that get there?'

'I wish no one was bothered about that.'

They all lost interest immediately. I scoffed the breakfast, and afterwards I felt a bit stodged out, but then I wished I felt fine, not full up but not hungry either, so that was all right.

The doorbell went, and it was Evan. There was a glow of happiness on his face. It's amazing the difference being happy makes to someone's face. You can't put your finger on it and say what feature's actually changed, but they just look *better* all round. Sharper. Brighter.

'How'd it go?' I said. 'With your dad?'

'Oh, Sam, it's just ... incredible. It's – I can't put it into words, it's like I had a ... terrible injury, and now it's healed. I'm just ... *so glad* he's like he used to be again! The doctors have got no idea how it happened! Thanks so much!'

'Oh, that's OK. No worries.'

Evan's face went thoughtful. 'There's not ... any sort of a catch, is there?'

'What d'you mean?'

'I mean, like, in stories when people wish, there's usually a catch. You know, it backfires, or you have to pay for it in some way.'

'Not with my wishes! I wish for it, I get it, that's it! End of.'

We walked on in silence for a while.

'What else are you gonna wish for?' Evan asked.

'Don't you want anything for yourself?'

'I guess.'

'What then?'

'I don't know.'

That was the problem. I really didn't know.

It seemed to me that other people had got a lot more happiness out of my wishes than I had, so far. And I didn't begrudge them that – in fact I got pleasure out of their happiness. But things I wanted for myself – well, it was just so easy to get them that it didn't seem to mean very much.

At school that day, for instance, I got top marks in Maths. Well, big deal.

I went along to the chess club at lunchtime and beat everyone there in simultaneous games, including Steve Rubenstein, who's played for the county. Again, big deal.

In PE we played football and I scored fifteen goals. Great.

In the afternoon I got bored in Science – I'd wished I understood everything about the parallax effect, so the teacher, Mr Qadir, was telling me stuff I already knew – so I just wished the bell would go an hour early.

Probably the best thing that happened at school was that Scorpus came up and said, 'Whatever you done to my old man, man, thanks! He's a different person now.' So that was good. But again, that was another thing I'd done for someone else. What about *me*?

After school I watched telly with Ben and made all the presenters say ridiculous things again. So on Blue Peter, when one of the presenters was trying to talk about a safari park where they were trying to get white rhinos to breed, I had the other presenter keep coming in front of her and singing 'My Old Man's a Dustman'. And then on Newsround I wished they'd report everything in sausage-and-mash – you know, that game where every time you get a word beginning with 's' you say 'sausage' and every time it begins with 'm' you say 'mash'. So this report about the European Space Agency became a report about the European Sausage Agency. And they said that the European Sausage Agency was hoping to put a sausage rocket on the mash, and they'd be able to find out a great deal about the mash of sausage. Then there was a quiz show and I wished one of the teams would answer 'custard' to every question while the other team answered 'bum'. It was pretty funny. Ben was in fits.

But.

The problem was that all this stuff was, like, trivial, you know? It was kind of fun – well, yeah, it *was* fun, let's be fair, but it was still sort of . . . unsatisfying.

I thought about it later that evening, as I was floating about in my bedroom (I'd wished for it to be zero-gravity in my room, just for a change) and drinking a ginger beer I'd wished for. At first everything – all the furniture and the ginger beer – went floating about the room as well, until I wished for it all to behave normally but for the room to be zero-grav just as far as *I* was concerned, so that was all right.

I still didn't know what I really wanted. The problem was, it almost didn't make sense to want things any more. Because how can you want something when you can just get it, immediately, just by asking for it? When there's no gap between wanting something and getting it, then getting it doesn't mean anything. There's no tension. No relief or surprise or sudden joy.

The most successful wishes, I realized, were the ones where I did good stuff for other people. Because when you unexpectedly get good stuff from someone else's wish, then it *does* mean something – there's room to feel surprise, relief or sudden joy. So maybe I should think of some more wishes to help other people?

And try thinking bigger. I mean, I could make Scorpus's dad a nicer person just by wishing for it. I could cure people with terminal illnesses! I shouldn't be wasting my wishes on making presenters on children's telly say silly things to make Ben laugh. With all the power I had, I should be doing something much more serious.

But . . . what?

And then I had an idea so big it took my breath away.

How about this: what if I wished that *everyone on Earth was nice all the time*?

People being polite and kind and generous to each other all the time. All over the world. Think about it. No more wars, no more violence, not even anyone being snippy or snarky or snitty or sarcastic any more.

That was certainly a pretty big idea. But as soon as I'd had it, I had *another* idea, and it was even more colossal, and took my breath away even more than the first one.

What if I wished that *no one would die ever again*?

Let's face it, the fact that everybody does have to croak it sooner or later is a major downer. But without death – no more funerals, no more orphans, no more grieving and mourning . . .

Plus everyone being nice . . .

That would be heaven on Earth, wouldn't it?

I didn't stop to think. 'I wish everyone on Earth was as nice as possible to everyone else all the time. And I wish people would stop dying.'

After that I felt a bit tired. It had been a busy day. So I wished my teeth were cleaned and I was lying in bed in silk pyjamas. I couldn't wait for the next day to see how my wishes had changed the world.

I closed my eyes, wished myself pleasant dreams, and wished to fall asleep in ten seconds.

CHAPTER TWELVE

'ood morning, Sam. You look good today!'
Maeve said.

'Do I?'

'Yeah, really handsome.'

'Thanks, you look really pretty.'

'You both look lovely!' Mum said.

'You all look absolutely wonderful!' said my dad.

'So do you, Dad,' said Ben. 'And you don't just *look* wonderful, you are wonderful!'

I chipped in. 'You're wonderful too, Ben!'

'We're all wonderful!' said my mum.

'Everyone in the world is wonderful!' Maeve said

– and at that precise moment, and I hadn't even wished for this, the radio started playing that old song by Louis Armstrong, 'What a Wonderful World', and we all burst out laughing.

The doorbell went ping and it was Evan. 'Hi Sam. It's so good to see you! You're my best friend and I really, really like you!'

'I really, really like you too, Evan!'

'Actually, I really like everyone!'

'So do I, 'cause everyone's really nice!'

'They are, you're right, that's totally correct.'

'So really, *everyone's* our best friend!'

'You're right, Sam! That's an incredibly perceptive comment.'

'Thanks. And you're incredibly perceptive too, Evan.'

On the way to school, total strangers kept smiling at us and calling out 'Good morning!'. We passed two drivers who were arguing, in the nicest possible way, about who should have a parking space – each one was trying to insist that the other one should have it.

At school, everyone was opening doors for each other and trying to get the other person to go through first. It created quite a few traffic jams in the corridors. Even Scorpus was being nice. I saw him carrying Tiffany Johnson's books for her, while jabbering on about how lovely and glossy her hair was. In Geography, Miss Skelmersdale gave us a test, but also gave out all the answers at the same time because, she said, she didn't want anyone to feel bad about not getting top marks.

At lunchtime I played football. I'd already made a wish to be brilliant at football yesterday, but today I wished everyone else was just as brilliant as me, otherwise they might get upset, and I couldn't bear that. It was sort of a peculiar game. Early on, I was running down the wing with the ball at my feet and Iqbal Patel moved in to tackle me. I thought I could maybe flick the ball past and run round him – but then, if I succeeded, he'd feel humiliated. No, it would be better if I let him tackle me, 'cause then he'd feel good about himself. I pushed the ball a bit too far forward so he had the chance to snatch it off my toes – but he slowed down and kind of waved for me to go past him. I stopped and made a sort of be-my-guest gesture, pointing at the ball.

'No, you go, bro.'

'No, it's OK, you can tackle me.'

'No, man, you keep the ball, you deserve it.'

'But so do you!'

We kind of smiled at each other. Iqbal said, 'Why don't we give it to someone else?'

'Yeah, you're right, it's good to share. Shall we give it to Evan?'

'Yeah, I like Evan, he's a good guy.'

'One of the best.'

I passed it to Evan (who was on Iqbal's team) and he ran towards the goal with it. As he got to the edge of the penalty area all the defenders melted away to give him a clear shot. And our goalie walked away from the goal and leant on the post with his arms folded.

He nodded pleasantly at Evan. 'There you go, it's all yours.'

All the defenders clapped this generous gesture.

'Go on, Evan!' I shouted. 'Stick it away!'

'No, I can't,' said Evan. 'Then it would be one-nil and you guys would be really upset.'

'No, honestly, we don't mind!' I said.

'Don't score, Evan,' Iqbal advised him, 'it wouldn't be fair on them.'

'You're right.' Evan carefully kicked the ball wide

of the goal. Now it was the turn of his own team to applaud.

The game ended in a nil-nil draw. It wasn't very exciting. But it was very good-natured.

When I got in from school, Mum was on the phone. 'No, I quite understand,' she was saying. 'I totally agree with you. I think this shows how sensitive and empathetic you are, and I admire you for it.'

'Hello lovely Mother. Who was that?' I asked, as she hung up.

'Hello darling Sam. That was the marvellous Bernard Souter. He was just saying he feels really guilty about all the artists he's ever given bad reviews to, and he wants to make amends. So he'd like to ask them all if they want to share my exhibition. I said yes, of course.'

'How many of them are there?'

'About five thousand.'

'Gonna be a bit crowded.'

'Yes – but think how hurt anyone would be if they were left out!'

'You're right, Mum,' I said. 'You're dead right.'

*

I was in the kitchen eating a seafood salad that I'd wished for when Maeve came in.

'Hello darling little brother.'

'Hi beautiful sister. Did you have a lovely day?'

Maeve started crying, but she was also sort of smiling through the tears. 'Yes, it was lovely, thanks, but . . . difficult. I had to tell Stefan he could go out with Josephine Waxwing again. She was so upset when he chucked her and I just knew it wasn't fair. She's such a nice person.'

'Oh, poor Maeve! So he's chucked *you* instead?'

'No, we came to an arrangement. She's going to go out with him on Mondays, Wednesdays and Fridays, and I have him on Tuesdays, Thursdays and Saturdays.'

'What about Sundays?'

'That's his day off. But I go out with Stanley Jollop then. He's fancied me for years and I can't bear to disappoint him. He's so nice.'

'Oh, good, so that's all sorted then. That was really clever of you.'

Maeve shook her head. 'I don't know, though – am I doing enough to make everyone happy? There may be other boys who want to go out with me too, and I can't bear the thought of disappointing them!'

'There's bound to be other boys who want to go out with you!' I said. 'Hundreds of them. Because you're so nice!'

'D'you think I should go out with all of them?'

'Well, it'll be difficult, but I s'pose you should . . .'

Maeve thought about this. 'I'll have to organize some sort of rota . . .'

A bit later, when Dad came in from work, he told us he'd invited Roger Haggerston and everyone else who worked in the building to share his office with the river view with him.

We all agreed he'd done the right thing. But it did occur to me that I'd created a pretty weird world.

And I wasn't quite sure how it was going to work out.

CHAPTER THIRTEEN

Normally I don't watch the news. It's either really boring, about things I don't understand, like politics and interest rates and the Eurozone, or it's full of horrible, scary stories about people getting bashed, beaten, brutalized, butchered or blown up.

I mean, frankly I don't know why they put it on. They're either mad or they think everyone else is mad. No one but a psychopath could enjoy it. And it's not just once a week, like most programmes, but every single day. Several times a day in fact. The whole thing's insane.

But what I'm leading up to is that on this particular day I did settle down on the sofa at six o'clock with a Coke and a slice of pizza and, just for a change, switched on the news. I knew no crimes would have been committed now that everyone was nice, so I was curious to see what they'd fill the programme with.

The newsreader, an Asian guy with a pink tie with purple swirls on it, was all happy and smiley. 'Today's extraordinary story, which is being confirmed from all around the world, is that, for the first time in human history, a day has passed on which nobody seems to have died, anywhere on the globe. Not one death has been recorded in the last twenty-four hours in any hospital in the United Kingdom. The story is the same throughout the European Union, and other countries are confirming the same remarkable phenomenon. Angela Crudgington reports.'

Cut to a woman with a mike, standing outside a big hospital with a stationary fleet of ambulances in the background. The wind whipped her blonde hair about her face. Another Asian guy in a white coat with a stethoscope around his neck was standing beside her. 'I'm at Whipps Cross, the largest hospital in East London, with a patient population of some three thousand people and many times that number of outpatients, as well as a busy A&E department which sees around two hundred patients a day. In a normal twenty-four-hour period, doctors say the hospital would expect to lose two or three patients. But no one has died since yesterday. A freak statistic – or evidence of something far more mysterious?

'I have with me the very charming, intelligent and handsome Dr Wickramasinghe – he really is a great guy, there's no question about that.' She pushed the mike under the doctor's nose. 'Dr Wickramasinghe – how do you account for this?'

Dr Wickramasinghe said, 'Thanks, Angela. I'd just like to say first of all that you are an extremely good-looking and talented interviewer! Well, we can't account for it at this stage. If this hospital alone was involved, I'd say we'd just had a good day – it's not unheard of to have a twenty-four-hour period in which no one dies. But two things make this very strange indeed. First, several colleagues have told me of individual cases involving terminally ill patients who really seemed unlikely to make it through this last day, but every single one of them has hung on.

But second, and this is the truly amazing thing, it appears that no hospital in the country or – and this seems frankly incredible – *in the world* has reported any deaths for this period. That's got to be more than just a freak statistic.'

'So what's your explanation?'

'That's a great question, Angela. But I don't have an explanation.'

'Could it be that, well, people have just *stopped dying*? We might all live for ever?'

'Well, that's impossible, of course.'

'So what's the explanation then?'

'I told you, I don't have one.'

The interviewer looked a bit kind of nonplussed. 'This is Angela Crudgington in East London. Back to you in the studio, Martin.'

'Thank you, Angela. I have with me the very intelligent and extremely nice population expert Dr Timothy Wendover, from the University of East Anglia.'

The guy with him looked like a typical eccentric professor, with a wild, unruly beard and a small pair of glasses which sat crookedly on his nose. 'Good evening,' he said. 'I really like your tie, by the way.

That's a very attractive pattern, good choice.'

'Thanks very much. It's really kind of you. So, Dr Wendover, this is something quite unprecedented, isn't it?'

'It is totally unprecedented. Usually, something of the order of forty thousand people die, worldwide, every *hour*. The idea that even for an hour nobody would die is frankly bizarre – and a whole day seems outright impossible. And yet that is apparently the case. Assuming these early reports are reliable. And they do seem to be.'

'So it has come as a total surprise – there were no indications of a decrease in death rates prior to this?'

The professor swept the suggestion away with both hands and his glasses slipped down his nose a bit further. 'Not *at all*. In fact, there has actually been an upward trend in deaths per day, as the world population continues to grow. This has come out of nowhere and we have no way of accounting for it.'

'Could it be connected with improved medical care – better medicines and hygiene standards . . . ?'

'That's a very smart suggestion,' said Dr Wendover. 'It was clever of you to make it and I hope you won't be offended when I say that can't be the explanation. In the first place, the change is far too sudden and extreme to be explained in that way. And in the second place, rates of illness and accident haven't changed. It's not as if everyone has suddenly got better. People who were terminally ill yesterday are still terminally ill. People all over the world were admitted to hospital after car crashes and other accidents, many with terrible injuries which would normally be fatal – but somehow *nobody died.*

That made me feel a bit queasy. I hadn't thought of that. All those people lying in intensive care who by rights should have been dead, hanging on to life when they maybe didn't even want to. That hadn't occurred to me when I made the wish.

'Some have suggested that something miraculous has occurred,' the newsreader was saying. 'That a profound change has taken place and humans are no longer mortal. It sounds far-fetched, I know, but could there be any possibility . . .?'

'Good question. You're right to pose it. An event as bizarre as this naturally encourages us to seek bizarre explanations. But it is of course impossible that we could have become immortal, unless the laws of biology have all been cancelled.'

'But suppose that had happened – would that be good news for the human race?'

Dr Wendover looked serious and sorrowful. 'You might think so, and believe me I understand why you might think that. But if true, that would be an utter disaster.'

I leant forward a bit. What did he mean, an utter disaster?

'You see, while death rates have stopped – at least temporarily – birth rates have not,' Dr Wendover went on. 'So the world's population would rise very, very fast indeed. Soon there would be food shortages. Water shortages. Shortages of resources. But still no one would die. People who were starving would simply carry on starving. But not dying. And because illness has not stopped either, you'd have lots of people suffering from disease, but the disease would never kill them. They'd just carry on suffering for eternity. It would, in fact, be hell on Earth.'

He was so upset by this prospect that he burst into tears.

So did the newsreader.

And so did I.

I'd screwed up with that last wish. Big-time. I

hadn't meant to cause all these problems.

Problems.

Problems.

Problems *were* the problem, weren't they?

A light bulb went on above my head.

What if there were no more problems?

Through my sobs, I said, 'I wish there were no more problems in the world!'

And then everything went quiet.

CHAPTER FOURTEEN

You're not normally aware of it, but there's always some kind of noise going on in the background, even when it's quiet. If there are other people in the house you hear them moving about or breathing, you hear the radio in a muffled kind of way from distant rooms, you hear the hum of the fridge, you hear sounds from the street outside, dogs barking, people walking past and cars vrooming along, etc, etc.

But now all that had stopped. Cut off, abruptly, as if someone had hit the mute button.

'Mum? Dad?'

Silence.

I went out into the hall. 'Maeve? Ben?'

No answer.

'Billiam?'

They'd all been in the house a minute ago. Maeve was up in her room, presumably on Facebook, Dad was having a bath, Ben was helping Mum cook in the kitchen (he likes doing that) and Billiam was hanging around their feet hoping they'd drop something he could eat ('If it goes to ground, it belongs to the hound', that's what we say in our house). But now they'd all disappeared. Where?

It was kind of freaky. I went outside into the street. Everything was there, as usual, all the houses with cars parked outside and bins in the front gardens. Clouds were slowly drifting across the sky, so it wasn't like everything had stopped moving. But there didn't seem to be any people. No birds sang. What was going on?

I walked into the centre of town. I didn't see a living thing. No dogs or cats. Not even any insects. I got to the High Street and all the shops were there as usual but nobody was in them. I stepped into Sainsbury's, and the automatic doors swished open to let me in, and there were all these aisles of fruit and vegetables and stuff, and there was rubbish music playing softly, but there were no customers and nobody on the tills. Not a soul in sight. It was kind of eerie.

I didn't like being on my own any more. 'I wish Evan was here.'

Evan appeared in front of me. I felt incredibly relieved to see him. But he looked seriously confused. 'Sam! What's going on? Where is everybody?'

'I was hoping you might be able to tell me. Where have you just come from?'

'I don't know! I was watching telly, that amazing news story about how everyone's stopped dying – and I was just thinking, I bet Sam's got something to do with this, and then everything went black. And now I'm here. Come on, what did you wish?'

'I wished there were no problems in the world.'

Evan's confused expression morphed into the lost-in-thought one. His hands went to his mouth. 'Right . . . that's quite a wish, Sam!'

'I s'pose it is,' I agreed. 'But how could it make everyone disappear?'

'Well, the thing is, there are always problems in

life, aren't there?' Evan said. 'I mean, there's got to be. Working out what's the best thing to do. Making choices. Dealing with stuff. But if there are no people – then there are no problems!'

'So it's like this all over the world?'

'Must be. That was the only way of making sure there could never be any problems!'

There was a pause as we both thought about this huge globe, completely deserted except for us two. Skyscrapers, street markets, sports stadiums, shopping centres, city squares, all as still and empty as the Sahara Desert.

'But what about all the animals?' I said. 'They don't have problems.'

'Of course they do! Say you're a cat, and you're getting bullied by the tomcat next door. Or you're a fox and you can't find any food. Or you're a slug and a hedgehog is trying to eat you . . .'

'Hmm. I guess . . .'

'The only way you could have a world without problems is if you had a world without life, right? Like, there are no problems on Mars, are there? 'Cause there's nobody there to have them!'

Looked like I'd messed up again.

'I know you're trying to help,' Evan said. 'That's 'cause you're such a nice guy. You want to make the world a better place. That's good.'

'That's really nice of you to say, Evan. You're a super-nice guy too.' I was starting to get a bit fed up with paying compliments all the time, but I couldn't stop. 'So, what you're saying – in the nicest possible way, because you're so nice – is that I've screwed up here?'

'Well, yeah, but I'm not blaming you, 'cause I know your intentions were good. Anyway, you can fix this, can't you? Unwish it?'

'Yeah. 'Course,' I said. 'But – I need to think. How to do it.'

'Yeah, it's a problem all right?'

As soon as he said that, I thought, *Oh, no, no, no don't*—

Then everything went black.

CHAPTER FIFTEEN

I seemed to be floating somewhere. Not like when you're floating in water and you can feel yourself bobbing up and down. In fact, floating's probably the wrong word. I only say that because my feet weren't touching the ground. I don't think there was any ground to touch. Everything was black. I mean, *really* black. I closed my eyes and opened them again and it didn't make any difference. I had no idea where I was, or if I even was anywhere. I was fairly sure I wasn't in Sainsbury's any more, but that was about all I *was* sure of.

'Evan?'

Silence.

'I wish I knew where I was.'

You are apart from the world, the Wish-Answerer said. It was a relief to hear that posh newsreader's voice again. At least someone was talking to me.

'I wish I knew why I was here.'

You wished for a world with no problems. But then you yourself faced the problem of what to wish for next. So you had to be removed from the world. To keep it free of problems. As you yourself had wished.

Well, that's exactly what I'd thought. Unless I wanted to spend the rest of my life dangling around here in the dark, I'd have to allow a few problems back into the world.

The wish about nobody dying – that would have to go too. We didn't want *that* many problems. And the wish about everybody being nice all the time – well, that had been, er, nice in some ways, but you couldn't really go on like that. Even just a day of it had started to give me the heebie-jeebies.

'All right,' I said to the Wish-Answerer. 'Here's what I wish. I want the world to go back to exactly how it was one second *before* I wished everyone was nice all the time and that people would stop dying, OK?'

*

The scene changed like a film cut. I was back in my bedroom, hovering around in zero-grav, holding a glass of ginger beer with a straw in it. It was about seven in the evening. I could hear the dog barking out in the garden. Downstairs, the telly was on and I heard the toilet flush in the bathroom. The world was up and running again.

I finished the ginger beer, positioned myself above the bed, wished for gravity to return to normal and plumphed down on to the duvet.

Right.

Now what?

It's fair to say I was feeling a bit frazzled. Events of the last few days had been a bit . . . *extreme*. I'd changed things so often and changed them back again that I hardly knew where I was any more.

I had almost infinite power, but in a strange kind of way I felt almost powerless. Because I no longer had any direct contact with reality – it wasn't like I was a person *in* the world any more, a person that could actually be affected by stuff that went on around me.

It was more like the world wasn't *real* to me any

more. It was a world of Lego, or Play-Doh, that I could just remodel however I wanted.

I'd turned the world into a toy.

People who lose contact with reality are crazy, aren't they?

Insane.

And I have to say I was feeling pretty insane at this point.

Maybe I should ask the Wish-Answerer what to do? He was the only person – if he *was* a person – who seemed to know what was going on.

I had a sudden urge for a personal interview.

'Wish-Answerer? I wish you'd come and see me.'

There was a sudden fierce heat.

This time he was his proper size: a rugged chunk of rock, about as big as a washing machine, standing there on skinny legs in the middle of my bedroom.

'I need some explanations, Wish-Answerer,' I said. 'What *are* you exactly?'

There is no word for the kind of being I am in your language.

'But you're alive, right? You're some sort of life form?'

I'm still not sure how it did it, since it was one big

chunk of rock, but the Meteor nodded.

'So you're not really a meteor?'

No. I merely resemble one.

'Why?'

You would not understand.

'And why – I mean, I wish you'd tell me why you gave me all those wishes.'

You would not understand.

'Well, tell me anyway.'

To renticufilicate the sparsunstrang of the universe.

'Oh. Yeah. Right. I thought it might be that.'

I said you would not understand.

'OK, look – whatever reason you did it for, you're on my side, right? You're here to help me?'

I do not take sides. But I am here to answer your wishes.

'I'm not sure I want the wishes any more,' I said, and as soon as I said it I realized it was true. Having all those wishes made life pointless. Even down to little things, like playing Top Trumps with Evan. It was no fun beating him when I knew what all his cards were. And the same went for football, or chess, or any game at all – there was no fun if you could just win without effort. Suppose I decided to run a marathon? As soon as I got tired I'd wish it was over, and I'd be at the finish line.

But it wasn't just sports and games. The whole of *life* made no sense. Life means struggling, learning, improving, practising – *achieving* things. But you can't *achieve* anything when you only have to wish for it. All those things I'd wished to be brilliant at – French and football and chess and Physics – I couldn't actually *enjoy* them.

I opened my mouth. 'I wish I wasn't brilliant at French and football and chess and Physics any more – only just as good as I used to be.'

To test myself I tried to think what the French for 'grapefruit' was, and realized I didn't know. So that was good. If I wanted to find out, I'd have to – well, find out.

But I hadn't solved anything in the long term. If you've got the wishes, you can't help using them. Nobody could resist it.

I took a deep breath, gulped and said, 'I wish I didn't have any more wishes.'

I cannot grant that wish.

'What? Why can't you?'

It is in direct contradiction to your first wish. You

cannot both have a million wishes and not have them. You wished for a million wishes. You must therefore have a million wishes.

'Then I wish I could go back in time to just before I wished for them and *not* wish for them!' I said. This seemed pretty cunning to me.

The Wish-Answerer gave a snuffling noise, as if it was laughing. *That's impossible,* it said. *A logical paradox.*

'Why?' I demanded. 'I wished to go back in time before and that was OK!'

But you did not wish not to have your wishes. That cannot be. If you did not wish for the million wishes, then the wish to return to an earlier time and not have them could not be granted – because you would not be able, now, to wish!

'What?' A sick feeling began to steal over me. 'But I thought I could wish for anything. I can break the laws of physics!'

But not the laws of logic, the Wish-Answerer said. *You have the wishes now, and there is only one logically consistent way to get rid of them.*

'Use them all up?'

That is correct.

'And how many have I had so far?'

One hundred and sixty-four.

Oh, well, wasn't that just terrific. That meant I had . . . actually I couldn't be bothered to do the calculation so I just wished I knew the answer: nine hundred and ninety-nine thousand eight hundred and thirty-six.

Well, nine hundred and ninety-nine thousand eight hundred and thirty-five, now I'd used one up on the calculation. But that was still a shedload of wishes.

By the time I'd worked my way through them I'd be a gibbering wreck. And what sort of mess would the world be in?

'Oh, all right,' I said, a bit moodily. 'You might as well go then.'

And the next instant, the Meteor was gone. No goodbye or catch you later or anything. Just . . . *pfft.* No more meteor, except for a slight aftersmell of smoke.

CHAPTER SIXTEEN

he sun was glowing above the trees, casting long, slanting shadows. I looked behind me and I seemed to be twenty metres tall again. Evan too. And Billiam's shadow looked more like a giraffe's than a dog's.

It was a mild evening, about eight o'clock. Soon it would be dusk. I had that sort of sweet/sad feeling you sometimes get on fine, quiet autumn evenings. The trees were turning from green to yellow, and a few leaves were already falling. It was Friday, so no school the next day. Me and Evan had taken the dog out for a walk, to discuss the Wish Problem. I'd just explained to him all about what had happened – 'cause of course he didn't remember any of that stuff about everyone being nice and nobody dying. As far as he was concerned it hadn't happened.

'So you just unwished it all?'

'That's right.'

'You're not – I mean, there's no danger you'll unwish about my dad being well again? 'Cause I couldn't bear it, really . . .'

'No, no, don't worry, I've got no reason to do that. What I need to do is get rid of the rest of the wishes without messing anything up too much. But nine hundred and ninety-nine thousand eight hundred and thirty-five . . .'

'That's a lot to get through,' Evan agreed. 'Can't you just think of some sort of pointless wish and keep making it, and run them down like that? Like, wish you were wearing a hat and then wish you weren't wearing it and then wish you were, and so on, till they run out?'

'Well, I *could* . . .' I was a bit doubtful if this was going to use them up fast enough. 'Lemme give it a try . . . I wish I was wearing a hat, I wish I wasn't wearing a hat, I wish I was wearing a hat, I wish I wasn't wearing a hat, I wish I was wearing a hat, I wish I wasn't wearing a hat, I wish I was wearing a hat, I wish I wasn't wearing a hat ...' I stopped. It felt weird, this hat settling on my head and then vanishing over and over again. I could just see the brim of it. It was blue.

Evan was looking at me and laughing. 'It looked like it was sort of flashing on and off – like the light on top of a police car.'

'Well, that's eight wishes down. Nine hundred and ninety-nine thousand eight hundred and twenty-seven to go. But how long did it take?' I wished I knew. 'Ten seconds. So it takes about a second to make a wish. To get rid of them all, that would take . . .' Again, I wished I knew the answer straight off. 'That's over two hundred and seventy-seven hours. Or about eleven and a half days, non-stop, without eating or sleeping!'

'At least you just used up another couple of wishes working it out.'

'Yeah, great, only nine hundred and ninety-nine thousand eight hundred and twenty-*five* to go. There's gotta be an easier way.'

'Can't you just use them up a bit more slowly? It

might take a few weeks, but . . .'

I shook my head. 'As long as I've got them I know I'm gonna use them. And every wish I make makes the world seem a bit more unreal and pointless. I'll go crazy, Evan. Truly.'

I picked up a stick and threw it for Billiam. He went capering off after it, stirring up piles of fallen leaves.

Fallen leaves.

'Why don't you—' Evan began.

'Shush!' I said, waving my hand at him.

Fallen leaves.

My mind went into overdrive!

'Evan,' I said slowly. 'I think I've got it.'

'What's the answer?' said Evan.

'It'll work,' I said. 'I'm sure it will.'

'What?' demanded Evan.

'Are you listening, Meteor?' I said. 'I want nine hundred and ninety-nine thousand eight hundred and twenty-four leaves to fall from the trees in this forest – and each fallen leaf counts as a wish gone. OK?'

OK, the voice of the Meteor said inside my head.

All around us, yellow leaves, detached by the

breeze, fell, swirling and twirling and twisting to the ground.

Evan drew in his breath. He looked at me and grinned. 'Oh, neat. Nice. Sweet.'

'Yeah, it was pretty good, wasn't it?'

I'd saved my sanity! I could live a normal life again!

Normal, but better than before.

Everyone in my family was happy. Maeve with Stefan Bumgarner and Dad with his new job and Mum with her art exhibition, and Ben with his nit-free scalp, magic helicopter and new-found reading ability.

Evan had his dad back in tip-top health.

And as for me, I still had a million quid stashed on top of the wardrobe.

'Just one thing though,' Evan said. 'You wished for nine hundred and ninety-nine thousand eight hundred and twenty-*four* leaves to fall. I thought it was eight hundred and twenty-*five*?'

'Oh, yeah, I'm keeping one wish in reserve,' I said. 'For an emergency.'